THE BIRDCAGE PAPERS

For Nuala.

PETER O'NEILL

THE BIRDCAGE PAPERS

First published by Peter O'Neill in 2022
Dublin
Ireland

Paperback	ISBN: 978 1 78846 255 6
eBook – ePub format	ISBN: 978 1 78846 256 3
Amazon paperback edition	ISBN: 978 1 78846 257 0

Produced by Kazoo Independent Publishing Services
222 Beech Park, Lucan, Co. Dublin
kazoopublishing.com

Kazoo Independent Publishing Services is not the publisher of this work. All rights and responsibilities pertaining to this work remain with Peter O'Neill.

Kazoo offers independent authors a full range of publishing services.
For further details visit kazoopublishing.com

Cover artwork © Gerard Nolan, 2022
Cover design by Andrew Brown
Printed in the EU

BOOK ONE

Shadows in the Garden

Contents

1

The Prisoner

None of us could remember the exact time Cat disappeared.

Nor the day for that matter.

Or if the sun was shining.

Or if it was raining.

Or if the bins were out.

She just vanished, long tail and all.

Cat was a law unto herself, always coming and going in that slinking, cowering way of most cats.

She was always elegant, her glistening fur shimmering like blue-black oil on water every time she glided around the corner of the living room. No matter what I was doing, I knew immediately she was there, looking at me with those deep slanting, yellow eyes. Dangerous eyes.

Yes, I knew what she was thinking.

Was I an enemy? No.

Was I a friend? Maybe.

Was I dinner? Most definitely.

Despite my misgivings, I admired her greatly, but I never really knew her well, even though we saw each other most days.

We didn't talk much, at least she didn't.

She would cast a brief glance in my direction and then with a nod of her head, she'd slide away, oozing contempt and scorn, her long tail wafting the air like some independent being seeking out targets for the mother ship. That brief glance was always enough to send a shiver through my old bones.

I've been around a long time. I've seen things happen in living rooms and dining rooms that would fry your hair. And kitchens. Don't talk to me about kitchens, the absolute worst of all. Imagine all the dangers that lurk in a kitchen: hot ovens, gas stoves, microwaves, coffee machines, not to mention sharp knives, and especially boiling water. The kitchen is a minefield. A death trap.

Cat spent a lot of time in our kitchen. Cats like to be warm, so what better place than a kitchen? I'm glad I don't have to live there myself. It wouldn't suit me at all, even though a bit of warmth would be welcome from time to time. But I can tell you this, Cat would be in charge, no matter where she found herself. I don't think Cat feared anything, especially not kitchens. Cat was a very cool cat.

Of course, I didn't find out until later that there was a cat flap in the kitchen door so that Cat could come and go as she pleased. No wonder she spent a lot of her time there.

And more importantly, we didn't find out until later again

that Cat was more sensitive than we thought. You should never judge a cat, or anything else, by its cover.

So when we discovered that something was wrong and Cat was no longer around, we called a meeting. When I say meeting, I'm afraid I may be misleading you a bit. Usually our meetings are raucous and loud, with no leadership or direction, and they hardly ever end in a resolution unless you count Mouse pouting, Dog growling and Cat ignoring everyone, tail in the air as usual. Oh, I haven't mentioned Mouse or Dog yet, have I?

I'll get around to that.

We called the meeting. Well, I called the meeting and in fact we had a very good one. But before we go there, maybe I should introduce myself first.

I am the Prisoner.

I'm completely innocent. I've never committed a crime.

'Yes,' I can hear you saying, 'don't all criminals say that?'

But honestly, never as much as a cross word have I spoken. You can ask anyone and I'm sure they'd agree. And remember this – I've never, ever been accused of any wrongdoing. I have never been brought before a judge or jury, never been arrested by the police. No criminal record at all, and yet here I am in a cage, imprisoned. And it looks like being a life sentence.

Oh yes, it's a nice cage, I'll give you that, fully equipped with all mod cons. I have a bath and a little purple ladder to exercise on, and even a mirror. I have a few chimes, hanging from the roof of the cage, but I don't like them. One puff of wind in the night and they jingle jangle until I'm wide awake. After that there's no going back to sleep. You're always waiting for the jingling things to jangle again. Of course, just to annoy you, they never do.

The funny thing is that I don't remember ever being anywhere else. But I must be from somewhere. I must belong to a world other than this wire monstrosity. I've heard about green jungles baked by the hot sun every day, where birds like me flit about in big-leafed trees, scooping up tasty insects by the dozen. Sometimes at night, when all about is deathly quiet, I imagine that I hear the noises. Jungle noises. Monkeys screaming, lions roaring, elephants trumpeting and birds of every kind singing. It might sound like screeching to your ears. To me it's heavenly music, and for a while I'm completely content, transported to a happier place. All of my six eyelids close and I drift into joyful dreams of my jungle families.

Usually that's when the wind blows and those annoying bells wake me up.

I look at myself in the mirror every day and I know I cannot be the only green bird in the world. I should say that I also sport a very attractive array of yellow feathers on my chest. And I admit I like to preen.

Yes, you've guessed by now, I'm a parrot. I know the others sometimes refer to me as a budgerigar, or worse than that – a budgie – but that's only because none of them can pronounce budgerigar properly. You'll see in the meeting reports that I'm always referred to as Budgie. Please remember, dear reader, that I am in fact a parrot, or maybe a parakeet. I'm not really sure what the difference is.

I try to ignore what people call me.

Sometimes that's a hard thing to do.

Anyway, enough about me. Let me introduce you to Mouse and a few others.

2

Mouse and Dog

Everyone likes Mouse. Even Cat likes Mouse. Now that's a surprise to most people. 'How can a cat like a mouse?' they ask.

Fair question. Stranger still, Dog and Cat get on OK too.

So our house is a happy home. That's not to say that we don't have our little disagreements and the occasional argument. Arguments never solve anything. What are they except attempts to force everyone to think the same way as you? And what does it matter what you think? It only matters to you. What does it matter if Mouse thinks his cheese is green and I think it's yellow? He's going to eat it anyway.

But Mouse doesn't especially like cheese. He just doesn't like something going to waste. He would much prefer the seeds in my feeder pot.

'I like the crunch, Budgie,' he'd say, 'and the health benefits, of course. What can I tell you? I'm particular about my feed. Green cheese just doesn't seem right.'

He is most certainly a clever little thing. He has figured out a route to my cage by climbing the curtain cords up to the curtain rail and then scuttling over to the glass cabinet, from where he just has to make a short leap. Long ago, he also worked out a way to open the lock on my door. I had decided to ask him sometime if he would show me how to do it but I'd never got around to it.

That was about to change.

Mouse likes to talk. When in the mood he will spout poetry and sing songs. That doesn't sit well with everyone, but it suits me just fine. I like to listen. You can learn a lot by listening. You don't learn anything by talking. But sometimes I like to talk too, as you'll find out.

When Mouse is bored and looking for someone to talk to, he visits me in my cage. He talks and eats all my seeds until late into the night, munching and chatting about this and that. I remember one night he had eaten so many seeds, washed down by so many gulps of water between so many tales of mouse folklore, that his little belly expanded so much he was in no fit state to negotiate his dangerous route home. I had to put him in the corner and hide him with a piece of the cloth that was used to cover my cage at night. Luckily no one noticed him, and he was able to escape the next morning when his little body had shrunk a bit.

On that occasion I was not best pleased with him because he left a heap of something behind which smelt a little nasty. Mice can be most inconsiderate, can't they?

My dear old friend has been around for as long as I can remember. He doesn't have any children, at least none that he ever talks about.

Now that I think about it, nor has Cat and neither has

Dog. And I don't either. None of us have children. Is that the reason we acted the way we did? Maybe.

Stories sometimes don't go the way you think they should.

Dog is a lovely old mahogany brown colour. He's getting on in years, putting on weight and has trouble with his eyes. He's big and broad in the beam, with a tail that has wagged at least one too many times. He wanders around the house, sniffing at things as if he were a police bloodhound, but in truth I don't think his sense of smell was ever any good. He talks very little. He sleeps a lot. He doesn't bark much. He growls occasionally but he's usually in good humour. He belches and dribbles all the time while he prowls around as if he's looking for something but has forgotten what it was. I like to watch him from my cage as he wanders around the living room, sniffing and poking his nose into every cushion he can find.

Then suddenly he'll stop and look up at me. I don't think he knows quite what to make of me.

'Budgie?' he says.

I nod yes.

'Cage no good?'

'Not really,' I say.

He shakes his head. 'Cages are not natural. Especially not for birds. Feeding you all right, are they?'

'Yes, Dog. I can't complain.'

He nods wisely but he always seems to be thinking of something else. Makes you wonder what goes on inside a dog's brain.

Mouse tells me it's the same with him. Dog always asks

him how the other mice are doing. Mouse always replies that there are no other mice.

Dog goes, 'Harrumph. Could've sworn there were loads of mice about the place. Are you the only one left?'

And Mouse, to be kind, says that he doesn't think so, but he can't find them and that he's still looking.

'Ah, that's good,' says Dog. 'Let me know if you need any help.'

You can see why we like him. Not a bad bone in his big body.

And then of course there are all those other characters who live outside in the gardens. Normally our paths don't cross much but some of them really helped this story, so I better mention a few.

We have a fishpond. Nice people, the goldfish who live there. They complain a lot about birds always trying to eat them. Not birds like me. Birds my size are way too small to trouble fish but I regret to admit that my bigger relations can be real pests for our goldfish. Not all birds are like that as you'll find out when you meet the sparrows.

Then there's Hedgehog. He's a spiky fellow. Best not get on his wrong side.

And I better not forget the field mice, although they don't play a big part in our story. Mouse can't stand them.

'Are they not cousins?' I ask, just to rile him a bit. He never answers, but if looks could kill!

The foxes of course will play a part. And a hooded crow! Yuck! I don't like hooded crows.

I've seen their eyes.

3

The First Meeting

I called the meeting. It would only be the three of us, obviously. Cat was missing. I thought she'd been missing at least three days, but Mouse said more like four.

Dog didn't know what day it was. 'All days feel the same to me,' he growled.

'Who would like to start?' I asked.

'I will,' said Mouse, chomping on my seeds. Mouse usually made sure he was safely installed in my cage during our meetings. He said it was because of Cat. A mouse could never trust a cat.

'What would the world come to,' he would ask, 'if a cat befriended a mouse? Chaos, anarchy, the end of the world as we know it. That's what would happen. We can't have that. Wouldn't do at all.'

So Mouse did his best to make sure the world remained on its axis and stayed safe and sound. Little did he know how events would soon change his point of view and that a mouse could indeed become a cat's friend.

'OK, Mouse has the floor,' I said. I usually have to take charge of the meetings, otherwise, as Mouse is fond of saying, chaos, anarchy and so on will ensue. Personally, I think they will ensue no matter who takes charge. Disorder is never very far off in our household.

'Right,' said Mouse, raising himself to his full height and standing in the middle of the seed dish, which I noted was now nearly empty. I worried that he might have overdone the eating, but he appeared fairly trim and confident. 'Cat is missing,' he said. 'Missing for maybe four days. Cat going missing is not unusual. Dog, you remember that last time, just before Christmas, she was off with some boyfriend. Didn't come back for ages. And when she did, what a state she was in! Just as well fur bounces back. I don't know what that boyfriend did to her. So, this is what I think – Cat has eloped.'

He sat down and scooped up the remaining seeds.

'Eloped?' Dog said. 'Are you sure? I was thinking that she might have lost her way. I was thinking that it was a simple question of sending out somebody to find her. I know she likes to search out her own cat company. That's normal, but do you think she'd just leave without saying goodbye? I don't think so.'

'I don't think she'd bother saying goodbye to me,' said Mouse. 'What do you think, Budgie? Do you think Cat would leave you a farewell note?'

That was a puzzle indeed. I didn't like to say that other alternatives were possible. Maybe Cat had met with an accident. Knocked down by a car. Fallen into a ravine or a river. The possibilities were endless.

But in the end we all knew what Cat was like. She would never allow anything to happen to her. She was too strong for that. Or so we thought.

I thought Mouse could be right. Cat had probably gone off with another cat. More than likely she'd show up in due course with a bunch of little kittens and we'd all have to make a big fuss of them. I hoped she'd be happy. We all deserve to be happy. Nobody more than us prisoners.

The meeting concluded on that note and we went to bed.

Mouse unfortunately couldn't manage the tricky balancing required to cross the curtain rod as his belly had swelled up once again. He slept that night in the corner under the mirror and snored his head off, keeping me awake. Between Mouse and those bells, I don't think I ever get a decent snooze.

Still, if he hadn't been snoring so loudly, I would never have heard the faint cry that carried across the night sky. A whimpering, pleading noise coming somewhere from the direction of the fruit garden.

I was awake all night, listening and wondering why the cry was so familiar.

I should have known.

4

Next Day

D og barked. Dog hardly ever barked. And Dog especially almost never barked at six in the morning. As I said, I was awake the whole night. The only time I managed to fall asleep was at the very moment Dog barked. I could have killed him.

Not really. Imagine a bird like me, big and all as I am, killing a dog. Especially a dog as big as our Dog. I examined myself in the mirror and ruffled a few of my yellow feathers. I looked good.

Dog barked again.

'What's the matter, Dog?'

'Can you not hear it?' he asked.

'The cries?'

'Yes.'

'Could be a fox. We hear them doing that from time to time.'

Dog shook his head. 'It's a cat. Definitely a cat.'

'Our Cat?'

'Yes.'

'Are you sure?'

'Yes.'

'Where's it coming from? The house?'

'No, the fruit garden.'

'The fruit garden?' I heard myself repeating.

The back garden is divided into three spaces. First there is the formal garden filled with the usual colourful flowers and evergreen bushes, where the noisy, smelly barbecues are held. There is the goldfish pond in one corner. Then behind a border hedge, there's an overgrown vegetable patch brimming with all the usual inedible green stuff that some people like, and beyond that the fruit garden full of apple trees, pear trees along the walls, with blackberry and raspberry brambles running riot everywhere.

'What's so special about the fruit garden?' I asked. 'We hear noises from there all the time. The place is full of birds and bats, all sorts of animals looking for something easy to eat. And insects! Big insects can make a lot of noise.'

But I knew he was right. I knew why the cries I heard during the night were so familiar.

'Well, this time it's Cat,' Dog insisted. 'She's in some sort of trouble and the trouble is just at the end of our garden.'

Oh, Dog, how wrong you were.

The trouble lay far beyond the end of the fruit garden.

He was right about one thing, though. Cat was in the fruit garden, curled up in a black furry ring, whimpering and crying and generally feeling sorry for herself. Dog found her hiding under a gooseberry bush, exhausted. She was lying on her side unable to go any further. He managed to coax her back onto her feet and nudged her gently back to the house.

I eventually succeeded in waking Mouse. I told him that we'd found Cat but she needed help. We all did what we could. I was useless. Directing operations from a birdcage is not ideal. In fact I have to admit I was no help at all.

Mouse wasn't much better. He scuttled this way and that, singing songs and quoting poems that were supposed to be appropriate to the situation but just made everyone depressed.

Cat was crying and making strange noises that made me uncomfortable and drove Mouse crazy. Thankfully Mouse stopped spouting the poetic stuff.

Dog was great. He calmed down Cat, licking and soothing her until she fell asleep.

'Is she asleep?' Mouse asked, crawling out from behind a cushion. No matter what, a mouse can never, ever trust a cat.

Nor can a bird. However, as I was safe and secure in my cage, Cat was never going to be a problem for me. Mouse, though, had to be careful.

'What's to be done?' he asked.

Dog shook his head. No ideas in there.

'What's the damage?' I asked. 'I can't be sure from up here but is that blood on her fur? Just there on her right leg.'

Mouse scampered over to check. 'Yes. A big scratch on her leg, not too deep. And look,' he cried, 'her ear is torn.'

'She's been in a fight,' I said.

'Wow, some fight!' Mouse was moving her leg to one side. 'Look at this.'

He held her famous tail in the air and showed us the wound.

Cat's tail seemed to be broken in two pieces, still connected, but bleeding. We needed to stem the flow.

'Dog, get some towels. Quick.' I hardly recognised my own voice, but I knew what had to be done. Sometimes it was very frustrating to be a bird. I knew what to do but I couldn't do it myself. 'Hurry, Mouse, fetch some wooden splints.'

Mouse looked puzzled.

'Something, anything to support the tail. Matchsticks would do, or ice-pop sticks might be better. Find something. Isn't there a cupboard in the kitchen with all sorts of bits and bobs in it?'

Mouse perked up. He knew where everything was. 'I'll be back,' he said.

'Bring some elastic bands too. Or Sellotape,' I shouted after him.

We wrapped Cat in warm towels. Mouse, who had returned with some wooden chopsticks, which Dog chewed in half, bound the two parts of the broken tail, straightening it with the sticks. They managed to hold everything together with elastic bands.

Not a bad job at all.

Then I noticed something peculiar about Cat's tail.

'Dog, would you hold up Cat's tail? Gently, please. We don't want to undo all our good work.'

Dog held her tail in the air and looked closely at it. 'Well, I never,' he declared, 'looks like she's lost a bit.'

Cat had lost about the length of my wingspan from the tip of her tail. That doesn't sound much but it would affect her balance and the way she carried herself.

All we could do now was wait. Cat was breathing easily.

The blood had stopped flowing and her shortened tail twitched weakly from time to time. If she didn't dismantle our makeshift splints, I reckoned she'd recover. The damage to her dignity might be a different story.

Mouse sighed. 'With that tail so short, it's going to be harder now to see her coming. I'll have to be more careful.'

And so, we kept a watch over Cat for the rest of the day. She slept soundly and we could see that with every breath she was getting better.

Little did we know though that Cat's story was far from over.

5

The Second Meeting

L ater that night, Cat was still sleeping. How I envy people who can sleep through anything. Cat was the best I had ever known. Thunderstorms, rain pelting against the windowpanes, lightning strikes or just a cup falling and smashing into smithereens on the kitchen tiles – nothing startled her. She was able to sleep through any calamity.

When she did wake up, she was able to walk and to eat. Her tail seemed to be on the mend and although she was still missing that large piece from the tip, Mouse's chopsticks, in the main, appeared to be doing their job.

We thought that was the end of it, but the next day when the mice started to come in from the fields, we realised that a profound change had come over Cat. She was not herself. She barely glanced at the field mice. Normally she'd be jumping and pouncing all over the little things, but now she showed no interest at all.

On the other hand, Mouse was getting extremely agitated. The field mice were overrunning his hidden stashes of food. He kept bumping into them while travelling down his winding warren of corridors behind the walls and the wainscoting.

I must admit that I was also getting concerned. It wouldn't be long before the little blighters found Mouse's secret trail up to my cage. I like my privacy, you see. I tolerate Mouse, but a horde of these little fellows – that would be too much.

So we called another meeting.

This time we had a full attendance.

Dog had dragged himself from whatever job he wasn't doing and sat patiently, waiting for us to begin.

Cat sat sullenly beside the fire, giving every indication that she wanted to be anywhere other than at this meeting. At least that was normal.

Mouse, as usual, was in my cage eating my food, less nervous now than he sometimes was. He could see that Cat was preoccupied, but not with him.

I made a note to myself to ask Cat what had caused her injuries. She might not want to talk about them, but if it meant that there was any danger to us, I felt we should know.

As usual, I had to kick off the discussion. 'We're here to talk about these field mice,' I said. 'It's getting worse. Every day there seems to be more and more of them. It's like a plague has hit our house. We must rid ourselves of them somehow. Mouse, you know them. Why are they invading us?'

Mouse swallowed a big seed and looked up in surprise. 'Me? Know them? They're field mice, for heaven's sake. I don't talk to field mice. I'm city. They're country. Good-for-nothing thieves and scoundrels, always looking for ways to interfere with city folk. Have you ever heard how they talk? That's to say, whenever they decide to talk to you. Might as well be listening to a Martian. Apart from that, I've nothing against them. Wish they were gone though.' Putting his head to one side, he whispered, 'Why don't you ask Cat? She should be hunting them down like the vermin they are.'

'Cat,' I said, 'what about it?' I was sure that she had heard Mouse's attempt at whispering. Cats have remarkable hearing.

But she said nothing and looked away. What was wrong with her?

I was about to address the elephant in the room and ask her, straight out, where she had been all this time and what exactly had happened to her, but before I could, Dog surprised us.

'I've had a chat with them,' he announced. 'They don't want to be here any more than we want them here, but they've no choice, you see. They said at least two foxes have shown up in the fruit garden and all the mice out there are terrified for their lives. Up to now, they haven't been too concerned about foxes coming into the garden and so they haven't built any defences to protect their homes. They are like an army in retreat and they prefer to take their chances with Cat. They're certainly not afraid of me – laughed, in fact, when I took a swipe at them. Not that I mind so much. They're nice little fellows.'

Cat stood up. She paced about the room, then stopped and looked at Dog, although I don't think she was seeing him. 'You said the foxes are here,' she whispered. 'The foxes have come to get me. What have we done? It's all my fault.'

We were all wondering what that outburst was about when suddenly a strangled, throaty bark broke the silence.

'A fox,' muttered Dog, 'and closer than the fruit garden, I bet.'

A long scream pierced the air and then everyone fell silent again.

Mouse whispered, 'They've killed their supper.'

'Yes,' said Dog. 'Hope it wasn't anyone we know.'

Cat suddenly ran from the room.

I had missed my chance to question her about those injuries.

6

Foxes

Before we go on, I would like to make it clear that I like all living creatures. I can't think of any I dislike. Well, maybe the people who put me in this cage. I can't bring myself to like them.

A parrot should be out there flying into the great blue and not trapped in a cage for the amusement of others. And so I do the only thing I can to fight against the brutal system of slavery, and rebel. If they ever want me to sing or say things like 'pretty Polly' or other such nonsense, I just clam up. Say nothing. Eat the seeds. And if I can, I'll poop some out just when they're not expecting it. Rebellion can take many forms, can it not?

Now, I myself have no fear of foxes. They're just like the rest of us. We all do what we must to survive.

The field mice have reason to be afraid of them, however. I understand that. They're on the menu. But Cat? Cat could stand up to a fox. They would hiss and snarl at each other and that would be that. Neither would want a fight. Neither would want to be injured.

And yet Cat was clearly afraid of the foxes.

She was already injured. I was thinking that it must have been the result of an encounter with the foxes. But why were they now in our fruit garden? What were they looking for? Were they still after Cat? It wasn't normal for foxes to hunt down a cat. After a fight they would lick their wounds and then go back to what really matters to them – finding something to eat.

What had Cat done that would cause them to behave like this? It must have been something really bad.

Cat had some explaining to do. I knew she was never going to answer to me or Mouse. Dog was the only one she might acknowledge as being anywhere near her equal. She might consider it worth her time to talk to him. So, with hope more than expectation, we asked Dog to have a word with her.

Dog managed to corner her and then cleverly manoeuvred her into a position just below my cage so that I could hear everything. He never ceased to surprise. Something must go on in that head of his.

Mouse, for a change, crouched beside the seed bowl and didn't attempt to eat a thing. More importantly, he stayed quiet.

I waited on my perch for Dog to start.

'Cat, what's going on?' he asked.

Good old Dog. Straight to the point.

And then we found out.

The Cat's Tale

Cat started talking, slowly at first, and then words surged from her like a raging torrent of water bursting through a dam. She couldn't stop.

I will do my best, readers, to convey her story in my words. Otherwise, you'd get confused.

The day she disappeared, which none of us could remember and which she couldn't either, was a bright, cheerful, sunny day and Cat was happier than she'd ever been because she was meeting a new friend. A special friend, she thought. He was handsome. Black like her, with a white streak down one ear and a white tip to his tail. She had met him a few times during her daily wanderings around the grounds of the house, and she had liked him.

'There you go,' said Mouse proudly. 'What did I tell you? Knew it all along. Boyfriend. Had to be. I said it.'

Dog and I told him to shut up, and he started sulking.

Then he began to eat my seeds again.

Cat took no notice of Mouse's interruptions and went on with her story.

She met up with her boyfriend at the river and spent the first day with him. They had a wonderful time together. She couldn't remember how long she had spent with him, such was her infatuation and her first experience of love. The days rolled by in a sweet fog that reduced the rest of the world to an irrelevance that merely changed from day to night and back again. She had sunshine twenty-four hours a day. And then they stumbled upon two young fox cubs playing by the river.

The cubs had been chasing each other around, and as fox cubs do, practising their pouncing and hunting skills on each other. When they saw the two cats, they decided to attack, not realising that cats would be inedible and, more importantly, that cats were quite a bit bigger than they were.

When Cat's boyfriend swiped his paw disdainfully and sent one of them flying through the bushes, it didn't deter them. On the contrary, they became more aggressive. Snarling and crouching low, they came in for the attack again, both concentrating on Cat's boyfriend. One of them managed to nip his leg, which changed his attitude entirely. Suddenly, his swipe turned into a fierce blow that sent one of the cubs into the river. Cat watched in horror as her boyfriend arched his back and made to pounce on the other cub.

'Stop! Don't hurt him. He's just a baby,' she cried.

Her boyfriend hesitated and the cub seized his chance to run away. The other cub was gamely clinging to a tree stump in the river. Clearly he was terrified and unable to swim.

'We've got to save him,' Cat said. 'He's going to drown.'

Her boyfriend showed no interest in the fox cub. 'I can't swim either,' he said. 'Serves him right anyway. Look what he did to my leg, the little terror.'

Cat hated the water too, but, ignoring her fears, she leapt onto the tree stump and crawled carefully along the log, which was moving this way and that in the current of the river. She eventually managed to reach the terrified cub and stretch out a paw to him. At first the cub was too afraid to let go of the log.

'Trust me. I won't let you go,' Cat assured him.

The cub was soaked and shivering. He looked more like a little water rat than a fox, his red coat stuck fast to his skin.

'I can't,' he gasped. 'My paw must be broken. I can't move it.'

Cat went further down the log than she wanted to. She dug her claws into the wood to hold herself firm, and then freeing one of her paws, she gripped the cub by his neck and hauled him up onto the trunk. Keeping him between her front legs, she managed to guide him back to the riverbank. They were alone. Her boyfriend had gone, and the other cub had not returned.

Cat's cub lay silently on the ground. His front leg was cut and bleeding. His neck was also bloodied where Cat had bit into him to drag him ashore. She licked the blood from his neck, trying to get him to stand and move about. He wasn't moving. He was getting colder by the minute.

Just then she heard a noise nearby.

The other cub strode out from beneath a bush. 'There's one of the cats,' he shouted. 'They killed my brother. Look at the blood. It's everywhere.'

Two adult foxes appeared from behind the cub. They were big and extremely angry.

'I tried to explain everything to them,' Cat told us. 'I tried to tell them that it was all a misunderstanding. I was saving the cub. But they didn't believe me, so I ran. They caught up with me, as you can see.' She looked ruefully at her broken tail. 'I'm ruined,' she wailed.

'But was the cub dead?' asked Mouse.

'I don't know. They kept screaming "Murderer! Killer!" I fought them off long enough to get away. Then I woke up in the fruit garden. I don't remember anything else.'

'What about your friend?' I asked.

Cat looked at me with deep sad eyes. 'He was here and now he's gone. I am on my own again. I've just got my friends.' She looked at each of us in turn.

I was moved almost to tears. Dog just garumpled but Mouse trembled and spilled his seeds all over the floor.

'I just didn't like the way she looked at me,' he said later.

'You never like the way she looks at you,' I pointed out.

'Exactly,' he said.

8

Questions

Telling her story had exhausted Cat. She rolled over and fell fast asleep. I told you she could sleep.

Mouse was the first to speak. 'Well, we know now why the foxes are in our garden,' he said. 'They're out for revenge. Glad I'm not in Cat's shoes.'

'Yes, you're right,' I said. 'The question is what can we do about it?'

Dog let out a big sigh. 'I'm surprised. Foxes don't usually go to this much trouble. There must be more to it than we know.'

'They thought Cat had killed their cub. Surely that explains it?' I said.

'Maybe. You can never tell with foxes. Wild, they are. Never became civilised like us dogs. They think they're superior to us, but they can't even bark. You've heard them scream at night like monkeys in the jungle. When all of us are trying to sleep, they're out there hunting and scavenging for food. No, you never can tell with foxes.'

'Could you talk to them?' I asked. 'Explain to them that Cat didn't kill the cub, that it wasn't her fault.'

'I'll try but I can't promise anything.' Dog hauled himself wearily to his feet and ambled towards the garden.

'Be careful,' I called after him. But I don't think he heard me.

'Mouse, do you think you could open this cage for me? I think it's time I broke out of jail, as it were. Time for me to stretch my wings and see if I can fly like I used to.'

'Course I can. Thought you'd never ask. What are you planning to do?'

The truth is I didn't know exactly what I was planning to do. I thought the key might be to find Cat's boyfriend and explain to him the trouble she was in.

It seemed from Cat's story that perhaps he didn't know what had happened. He left before the foxes had turned up. Maybe I could persuade him to come back, and together they could confront the foxes and explain their side of the story.

But why would he just go off like that? Without a word. No goodbye. It didn't sound right to me. Was he afraid of something?

And what about the dead cub? Was it the cat's strike that had killed him?

Was he even dead? We knew that he was alive when Cat dragged him from the water. He was complaining about a broken paw.

So many questions.

Mouse was busily poking and chewing at the lock on the

cage's door. Soon I'd be out there flying in the clear blue sky. Would I be able to do it? Would I be able to survive in the wild? I don't mind admitting, I was nervous about what lay ahead, but a part of me was excited too. I took a look in my mirror. Surely I would be fine. I was a big fellow, after all. I filled the whole mirror with green and yellow.

Magnificent.

Mouse broke my thoughts. 'Door is a good one, Budgie,' he said. 'Ready to go when you're finished plumping your little feathers in that mirror of yours. Can you remember how to fly?'

I wasn't ready to go yet. I wanted to see if Dog would return with any useful information. After what seemed like hours, he finally came back and plopped himself down below the cage. 'Can you hear me?' he called.

Mouse and I said we could.

'Well, I got to talk to the foxes if you could call it that. Talking isn't their strong suit. Much better at screaming and suchlike. I tried to explain Cat's side of things, but they weren't having any of it. They kept calling her the Shadow.'

Mouse raised his eyebrows. 'The Shadow?' he whispered.

'Seems there've been night-time attacks on their cubs by some other creature that they can't identify so they're calling it the Shadow,' Dog went on. 'This Shadow thing attacks at night when they're out foraging for food and their cubs are at their most vulnerable. I'm afraid their judge and jury have decided. Our Cat is the Shadow as far as they're concerned, and now that they know where she is, they're never going to let her go. They've sent word out to foxes everywhere. We can expect more to come before the day is out. They're taking this very seriously. I don't like it.'

'So they've decided the Shadow is a cat. Is there any doubt?' asked Mouse.

'No. They always suspected a cat or something like a cat. The foxes have never actually seen the Shadow, but they've seen what it's left behind. They've lost several cubs. Seems he or she only attacks the cubs. Yesterday was the first time a survivor had escaped to tell the tale. Truth is, I feel sorry for them. If our Cat has been prowling about killing foxes, then she's brought this on to her own head. I don't think we can protect her. I don't like it, but I can't see any other way.'

'And if she's innocent?' I asked.

Mouse was not helpful at this point. 'Who's innocent?' he asked, spitting out more of my seed husks. 'No one's innocent.'

'I don't know,' was Dog's reply.

Well, I had a pretty good idea. This Shadow fellow was most definitely not our Cat. There was a good chance that he was Cat's friend. That could explain why he disappeared like that. He knew the two cubs would cause problems for him. And it was during daylight. The Shadow operated only at night-time. He had lost his temper with the cubs and shown himself for what he really was, so he had to get away before anyone recognised him.

I knew now what had to be done.

9

Freedom

When freedom came, it wasn't what I expected.

I climbed up to the door of the cage and pushed it open.

'There you are,' said Mouse. 'Are you sure you know what you're doing? Are your wings up to this flying business? You know it's been a long time since you've actually flown. You might suddenly find you've lost your head for heights.' He kept blathering on about the door and the cage and the seeds.

'Mouse, you are a blithering idiot. I'm a parrot. I have a pair of beaks that will cut through anything, and I can fly like the best of them.'

Mouse started to chuckle. 'Have you looked into that mirror of yours recently?'

I didn't know what he was talking about. 'I look in the mirror every day,' I said. 'Is that a crime? What do you mean?'

'Nothing, nothing at all.'

I stayed silent. I've found that silence is a great way to get other people to talk. Sure enough, after a few minutes, Mouse said, 'Just saying that the mirror in your cage is magnifying. I nearly died when I saw myself in it that first time. Thought I was a hippopotamus, I did. Scared me almost to death, it did. What a laugh!'

I don't mind admitting that this came as a big shock to me. I climbed onto the mirror ladder and looked again. There I was, a big parrot. Plain as day.

'You're not as big as you think you are,' Mouse said. 'I just didn't want you to go out there on your own thinking you were this great big parrot, you know. You could get hurt. We don't know what's out there.'

I knew he meant well but I had to explain. 'I'm a parrot. And that's a fact. Maybe I'm not that good at explaining things but facts are facts.'

Mouse chuckled. 'Budgie,' he said slowly, as if I was stupid. 'Yes, you are a parrot. We all know that. But you're also a budgie. Same bird, but smaller. A lot smaller. Just remember what size you are when you get out there. Don't throw yourself against any of those big birds like pigeons or magpies or worse still, those hooded crows.' Mouse shuddered and shook himself. 'You won't stand a chance, especially against the crows. Wouldn't surprise me at all if one of those fellows was this Shadow geezer and not a cat at all.' He paused to let that thought sink into my empty head.

'Just remember, you'll have to use your colours to merge into the trees and flowers. Just like a soldier wearing camouflage. It's a wild world outside this cage. I don't know what you're planning to do but we'd like to see you back here soon. Besides, what would become of me without all those seeds of yours?' He spat the one husk of a seed from the side of his mouth. It pinged off the mirror and I saw my image bounce back and forth against the cage's bars. He was getting eerily accurate with these shots.

But Mouse was right – this wasn't going to be easy. And he didn't even know what I was planning to do. Then I realised that I didn't know what I was planning to do either. I needed help. I stood there by the cage door and tried to see what lay before me. I looked at the cage door and gasped with fright. How was I going to fit through that? It was way too small. I pushed my head through the opening and froze. It was quite a drop to the floor below. Just as well I can't fit, I thought, relieved that I didn't have to go through with it after all. Then from behind, Mouse launched himself towards me, hitting me in the tail just as I was turning to come back in. I was thrown out of the door of the cage and fell headlong through the air, frantically flapping my useless wings. I heard Mouse go 'Oops!' and shout in panic, 'Fly, fly, fly away!'

But I couldn't. I fell straight down and landed on Cat.

10

The Unlikely Brotherhood

For a moment I didn't know what had happened. Luckily the landing was soft. I rolled off Cat and onto the floor. I heard Mouse scrambling down the curtain cord, shouting at the top of his voice. 'No, no, no!' he was screaming. 'Dog, Dog, where are you?'

I was a little shaken but otherwise OK.

The problem Mouse had seen, and which I didn't yet realise, was that my fall had placed me directly beside Cat's gaping mouth. When I looked up, I could see a yawning cavern lined with sharp white teeth and a big pink tongue licking me up and down, making slurping sounds and spraying me with a shower of cat saliva.

'Budgie,' Cat said, 'at last you're up close.'

'Is that a good thing?' I stammered.

All the time I was trying to back away a little. I had still not fully recovered from the shock of my fall, but instinct had kicked in. I needed to put some distance between Cat and me.

I knew it would be useless. A single swipe and I was toast. There was no point in trying to escape. I had to talk my way out of the situation.

'A good thing? I don't know good things from bad things any more,' Cat said. 'Is it a good thing to fall in love?' she asked.

I didn't immediately reply. I was too busy getting as far away as I could. I knew it wasn't going to make a difference but instinct and adrenalin make a powerful concoction.

'I think it's a good thing to fall in love,' I said, 'unless you fell in love with a tree or the moon or some such thing. That wouldn't turn out so good. Don't you think?' First rule of engagement with the enemy – try to distract them.

Cat looked at me and I looked back and held her yellow eyes. I didn't know what she was thinking, but if I was to be her next meal I wanted her to remember me, not for my taste, which she'd forget in seconds, but for my character. So I held her yellow gaze. I didn't blink one of my six eyelids.

And then Cat chuckled. 'Don't worry, Budgie, I'm not going to eat you. We can't say the same about those foxes though, can we?'

'That's what I wanted to talk about. I've heard the story. The foxes think you're this Shadow fellow but you're not, are you?'

'No, I'm not.'

'That's good enough for me. Now we just have to prove it.'

Cat scoffed at me. 'Prove it? When the foxes are just outside our door, wanting to tear me apart. How are we going to do that?'

'I don't know yet. But I have an idea. You may not like it, but I think it's our only chance.'

Just then Mouse came scampering around the corner into the room, tail up, all anxious.

Dog lumbered in and pushed his wet nose into my face. 'You okay?'

'I'm fine, thanks.' I threw my best malevolent glance at Mouse. 'Thanks for throwing me out of the cage.'

He bared his toothy grin and said, 'Told you to look out. Said it was wild out there and you're not even out there yet. Lucky you fell on Cat.'

We all looked at Cat. Dog looked at me. I looked at Mouse. Mouse said, 'What?'

I had to say something. 'Can I say something?' I asked.

Three pairs of eyes looked at me.

'Here's what I think. First, we have foxes at our door. They want to kill our Cat. Our Cat is innocent. What are we to do? Run away and let these bullies decide what's right or wrong, what's true or untrue? Are we to live under the …'

Mouse stopped me. 'Budgie, just explain the plan.'

Sometimes I get carried away. 'I'm sorry, Cat, but I think your friend that you fell in love with must be the one the foxes call the Shadow. The only way to clear your name is to find him and bring him here to explain himself. The foxes have a right to know who it is that's killing their cubs.'

'No chance of that. He's well gone,' Cat said.

Good, I thought. She's over him. Or nearly.

The solution lay behind enemy lines. That job was for me and Dog. Cat would have to hold the fort here in the house.

Assuming he was the Shadow, the first thing we needed

to do was to find Cat's boyfriend. 'And if we can't find him, we'll have to find another way to prove Cat isn't the killer.'

Everyone nodded their heads in agreement.

'So we've got to organise ourselves. Let's imagine that we're an army. I'm ready to fly out, be the air force and scour the countryside looking for the Shadow. Dog will be my infantry. I'll send for you when I find him, Dog. Mouse, you can be intelligence. You know everyone. Ask around and see if we can pick up a trail.

'Cat, you'll have to lie low, out of sight. You mustn't let the foxes know where you are until we can prove your innocence. Keep a lookout. Stay alert and don't doze off like you always do. And you'll have to stay in the house. The foxes won't come in here.'

I just wanted to give Cat something to do. I was beginning to think that her attention span wasn't much longer than that of a goldfish, and I wasn't expecting much from the intelligence department either.

'Are you ready?' I asked.

'Yes,' they all said.

Dog's face garumpled. 'Looks like we're an army then, a real Band of Brothers,' he mumbled. 'I've heard it all now.' He looked at each of us in turn and shook his head sadly.

'I'm sure he's miles away by now,' sighed Cat.

11

The Gardens

What a day that was!

I flew through the living room and collided with what I now know are the patio windows. Mouse helped me climb back up to the cage.

'You need elevation in order to fly,' he kept saying.

How a mouse could know anything at all about flying was beyond me. I suppose he must have learnt something from all those books he spent his time nibbling. 'You won't be able to lift yourself off the ground, at least not yet. You need to strengthen those wings. Get them flexing again. You're out of practice.' He had persuaded me to stand on top of the cage. I was afraid to look down. If I wasn't able to fly, then all my plans would be for nothing.

'OK,' Mouse said. 'Ready, steady, goooooo!'

'Don't push me,' I yelled.

'I'm not pushing. Just let go!'

I closed my eyes and jumped. I could feel myself falling again and I kept flapping my wings as hard as I could. This time I didn't hit Cat or the floor. I kept walking through the air. Through it and on it. Over it, under it, behind it, sliding on the side of it like a surfer on a sea wave. It's the greatest, most exhilarating feeling in the world, surfing the airwaves.

Until you hit the patio windows!

That fairly knocked the stuffing out of me. 'Another good lesson,' Mouse advised, 'is to keep your eyes open when you're flying. Now, up you get and we'll try it again.'

I wanted to kill him but I knew he was right. I had to try again. I was nearly there. I felt ready to fly this time.

And I did.

Everything clicked into place. I was easily able to find my way around the room, picking out landing spots and practising my landing technique. I felt strong. I felt I could go even faster but the room was too small for that. I could do that later when I got out into the wide open spaces of the garden.

But first I had to find a way out. The patio doors were closed and so was the window.

'Mouse,' I pleaded. 'This isn't going to work if I can't get out. How can we open the patio doors? You're not thinking that I can fly up the chimney, are you? I don't think I want to do that.'

'You don't have to do that, Budgie. Dog knows all the doors that open to the outside, and besides, we have the cat flap in the kitchen. How do you think all those troublesome field mice got in?'

Of course, I thought, the cat flap in the kitchen. Dog

pushed open the door and led me to it. As I said before, I don't like kitchens. The sooner I was through the cat flap and away from all those sharp knives and microwaves the better.

It turned out that the cat flap was just a little swinging door, low down in the back door. I had never seen one before. I could see how the field mice had made use of it, but I wasn't too happy about flying through it. Suppose the flap swung back at me just as I was flying through!

I was pondering this dilemma when Cat strode forward. 'Here you go, Budgie,' she said, and she pushed open the flap door, holding it steady on her back. 'Have you room enough to get out?'

It looked wide enough for me. 'Thanks, Cat. I think I'll manage.'

I flew straight out and found a landing spot on a willow tree. From there I was able to get a good look at the garden, which I had never been able to do from my cage. I saw it stretch out below me. In the first part there was a path leading to a large pond with decorative rockeries. This was the formal garden. Beyond it a hedge separated the space set aside for vegetables, which was laid out in neat rows of greens and beans. There was a shed of some kind at the side of the house. Then another hedge and the fruit garden beyond that. I was too far away to see anything in there, but I was sure a fox or two lay hidden behind that hedge. I decided to investigate the pond. It was thirsty work this flying, and besides the chance of a drink, maybe I'd meet the goldfish.

I flew down and dipped my feet in the pond. I looked at my reflection in the water and felt really pleased with myself. I was free. I was out flying in the world, away from that boring cage.

Suddenly a big yawning mouth burst up from the depths and squirted a jet of water at me. I was drenched and shocked, two sensations I'm not very comfortable with.

The mouth disappeared only to be replaced by another and then another. Soon several pairs of eyes were studying me intently.

'Are you the budgie?' one of the mouths asked. 'We've never seen a green and yellow bird before. You're a pretty one.'

I didn't know whether to take that as a compliment or not. I wondered if a fish could eat a bird. Unlikely, I thought.

'We've heard all about you,' another mouth said excitedly.

'From where?' I asked, feeling a little paranoid. I was talking to fish, after all. I didn't do that every day. In fact, I'd never done it before.

'Oh here and there, everywhere. Most of the creatures living around here stop by the pond for a drink and a chat. Not much we don't know. For instance, there are two foxes in the fruit garden and they're up to no good. Bet you didn't know that. You've got to be careful if you're planning on going in there, but you should be able to stay out of their reach.'

'Unless they're flying foxes,' chipped in another goldfish, and a ripple of water shivered across the pond as they all burst into a hearty chuckle. Flying foxes indeed!

'I'm looking for a cat,' I said. 'A black cat with white markings on one leg and on his tail. Have you seen him? Has he been around here at all?'

There was a rumble of fish chatter and then another voice said, 'Yes, we've seen him. A few days ago. He was taking a drink from our pond and looking for Cat from the house. A nasty type. We didn't tell him anything. Haven't seen him since.'

'Do you know where I might find him? It's important.'

'No idea. But you should certainly avoid him. He was up to no good.'

'I have to find him,' I said.

'Well then, your best bet is to look for Hedgehog. He knows everyone here.'

The goldfish didn't know where Hedgehog might be but they told me to look along the hedge on the western side of the garden. I might have to travel as far as the fruit garden to find him.

'One more thing,' I asked. 'Do you know if there are any cubs with the foxes in the garden?'

The goldfish couldn't be certain, but they didn't think there were any cubs.

I just hoped these foxes weren't the flying kind.

The goldfish had made me nervous – nervous and paranoid. Not an ideal combination.

12

More Friends

I thanked the goldfish and headed off to find Hedgehog. It soon became apparent that it wasn't going to be easy to track him down. I realised that I had no idea what a hedgehog looked like. That was something I should have asked the goldfish. I settled on top of the hedge and looked around. Nothing in sight. Then suddenly on the ground beneath me a brown bush moved. I froze. Then the bush moved again. I looked at it. A brown shrub, covered in little thorns. Then two eyes peeked out from behind the thorns.

'Who's a pretty Polly then?' a shrill voice cracked through the air.

'Who's asking?'

'Why, I'm Hedgehog. Everyone knows that. This is my garden. I might ask you what business you have here?' The voice had risen an octave.

'Actually, I'm looking for you. I think you may be able to help me. I hope so anyway.'

Feeling a little foolish to be talking to a bush, I explained who I was and about Cat's problem with the foxes.

The bush unfurled itself, and as well as the eyes I could now make out a pointed nose and two small ears. He was a little animal not unlike a mouse except covered all over with little spikes and slightly bigger.

He peered at me and then his eyes widened as if he had suddenly realised who I was.

A prickly customer but his voice had calmed down a fraction.

'Ah, buddy,' he said. 'You're Dog's friend, aren't you? How is he? We haven't bumped into one another for a while, him being half blind and me being so short-sighted, I suppose. We keep missing each other on our travels. Still, a real gentleman the old fellow is. How can I help you, buddy?'

He kept calling me buddy and I didn't have the heart to tell him that I was Budgie.

'I'm looking for a cat. A black cat with white markings on his leg and tail.'

'I know the fellow,' Hedgehog replied immediately. 'Used to hang about down by the river near a big old log but I don't think that he's there now. A nasty piece of work. What do you want him for? I'd steer well clear of that rascal if I were you.'

It seemed nobody had a kind word for Cat's boyfriend. Whatever had she seen in him? There's just no accounting for taste.

There was still a chance that I'd be able to track him from the river, even if Hedgehog thought that he wasn't there anymore.

'Where's this river?' I asked.

Hedgehog gave me directions. I thanked him and made to move off.

'If you find him, don't tell him that it was I who told you,' he called out to me. 'I like a quiet life, I do, so don't tell him anything or …'

I didn't hear the rest. I was anxious to be on my way and I was already thrusting myself at great speed from the hedge. I suppose I was a little rude but today was not a day for socialising.

The river lay beyond the end of our garden. Hedgehog didn't know how far it was but according to him it was 'at least four days' walk'. I reckoned I could make it in fifteen minutes. I was wrong. Less than four minutes later I was looking at it. Hedgehogs must walk very slowly.

I had followed the western hedge until I was past the fruit garden and out into open marshland, which was pockmarked with brambles and a few large trees. I turned to the east and followed the river until I saw the broken tree lying across it, just as Hedgehog had described. This must have been the tree that Cat had crawled onto to save the fox cub. I could now see how she had managed to do that. Brave Cat.

I perched myself on the broken tree and looked around. No sign of life. No sign of any creatures living nearby. It was depressing to have come this far and have nothing to show for it, nothing to bring back to the house. I had failed. I was just about to turn around and head for home when I heard a faint, whirring sound and then a dark, enormous shadow spread across the marshlands in front of me. The whirring sound became louder and louder. My heart started beating frantically against my chest and I gripped the little twig I was perched on so hard that it broke in two and I fell, flapping and flailing, to earth. The Shadow, I thought, it has come for me. How stupid to think a little bird like me could make a difference. I closed my eyes and waited for the worst.

The shadow disintegrated into fragments of itself and noisily came to rest all around me. Then, only silence. Nothing happened.

I opened my eyes and all around, gazing with interest at me, was a flock of fifty or more birds. They were about my size, but their feathers were a dull brownish colour. They had no style at all. But they jostled and joked with each other, pointing at me and giggling.

'You've a lot of colour,' one of them said.

'Chuckle, chickle, chackle,' went fifty voices in reply.

'Just the usual colours for a budgie,' I said.

'Chundle, chandle, chindle,' rippled through the crowd of birds.

They were friendly and curious, and we chittered-chattered like this for a while. I found out that they were sparrows. A group like this called themselves a tribe.

They asked if I was alone. They couldn't understand how any bird could survive on its own and they became quite concerned for my safety. They began showing me how to scoop up insects while on the wing and how to get at seeds in the plants and gorse. One or two kept bumping into me and saying how beautiful I was. It was very distracting in a nice way and I won't say that I wasn't tempted to forget the whole Cat business and fly away with the tribe. But I didn't.

I asked them my usual questions and got the same replies.

Yes, they knew of a male cat with the white-tipped tail. No, they didn't know where he was. Yes, they had heard stories about a Shadow who had been causing some trouble among the foxes. That was why they couldn't understand why the foxes were in the fruit garden.

'What do you mean?' I asked.

'Well, they've left their cubs in their den. It's not that secure. If the Shadow is about, they'll be easy prey.'

This was news indeed. Cubs in a den. I had to talk to them. Could the cub we had supposed dead still be alive?

'Can you show me where they are?'

'Of course,' the tribe chackled in one voice.

That was not the only thing the tribe did as one. I found myself flying at great speed through the air with fifty companions, now part of a tribe of sparrows. What a day I was having!

And it wasn't over yet.

13

The Den

The sparrows didn't seem to have a leader. They just swarmed through the air with no obvious pattern to their flight, each doing their own thing and miraculously managing to avoid any mid-air collisions. I wasn't so confident. I was afraid that I wouldn't be able to fit into the flying formations of the tribe and even though I had great confidence in my new aerial skills, there was no guarantee that I wouldn't bring the whole flock down by some silly manoeuvre.

I made sure to keep well behind the rest of the birds and followed carefully as they made their way downriver. I kept an eye out for any strange movements either side of the riverbank, but there were none.

We tacked across the sky like a sailboat that must catch every gasp of wind in order to keep moving. Unlike a sailboat we birds don't have to search for wind in order to fly. If it's there, we take advantage of it but if there's no wind we just keep flapping our wings. There wasn't a breath of wind today and I wondered why we were making all these manoeuvres. Then I saw some crows circling to our right and I knew what the tribe was doing. Flying this way and that was all about confusing the enemy. The tribe had nothing to fear from the wind. Crows were a different matter. I was learning.

We left the crows to do whatever it is crows do, and with a gentle whoosh of air we came to rest on bushes and trees at a bend in the river. If our enemies were sparse in the skies, they were legion on the ground. We stayed in the trees. The birds chattered loudly among themselves as if they hadn't met for years. The silence of our little flight was over.

'Is this it?' I asked the bird next to me. I still couldn't distinguish one brown sparrow from another. 'I don't see any cubs.'

'Just wait a while. They're there all right. Just don't want to show themselves. Can't blame them either.'

We waited. I could see nothing and there was no hint of any movement on the ground. But it wasn't long before a small head appeared from beneath a bush. A fox cub. The chatter and conversations of the sparrows continued. I kept my gaze on the little head. It looked this way and that, unsure of what to make of the cacophony of bird noise that had suddenly invaded its hideaway.

A fox cub has no fear of small birds like us. Soon he was crawling out from under the bush and into the open. A brash, confident fellow who gave the tribe hardly a glance.

Then another head appeared. Another cub. This little fellow didn't look at all well. He stumbled behind the other cub, keeping close to what I assumed was his brother. I wondered if these were siblings of the cub Cat had tried to save.

The stronger cub began to push his brother away and then playfully pounced on him. The stumbling cub showed no interest in rough and tumble, much to the frustration of the stronger cub. He just lay down and sighed deeply.

I took my opportunity. I had to speak to these fellows.

'Now then, you guys. What are you playing at?' I decided to put on a stern voice. After all, these were children. They'd pay attention to a serious adult like me. I hoped.

They looked around, startled. Was a bird speaking to them? That was unexpected. It didn't take them long to home in on me. My yellow and green feathers stuck out among all the brown perched on every branch around.

'Who are you?' they asked.

For what seemed about the fiftieth time that day, I explained who I was and what I was looking for.

The little cub became agitated and began pulling his brother's tail. 'Tell him,' he said.

The other cub said nothing.

'Tell me what?' I asked. My voice had become gentler. These cubs were afraid of something. I didn't want to frighten them away.

'Do you know the cat?' they asked.

'Depends on the cat,' I said. 'I have a good friend who lives in the house beyond the fruit garden. A black cat. She's been in some trouble with foxes.' I waited for a reaction.

The cubs looked at one another. 'Has she a white tail?'

'No. All black. But she's missing a bit and that's what I'd like to ask you about.'

The big cub hissed. 'She's the cat who nearly killed my brother. My parents will tear her to shreds, you'll see. They're at the house now. They have that piece of her tail and when they match it to your friend's tail, they'll kill her, and good riddance. Once she leaves the house and shows herself, they'll know.'

The other cub looked downcast. He didn't look at me.

'Is that what you think?' I asked him.

His brother jumped in quickly before the little fellow could reply. 'Of course it's what he thinks. What else would he think? That cat nearly killed him. Look at him. He's not better yet.'

I kept my eyes fixed on the small cub. 'The cat that nearly killed you. The cat that threw you into the river had white markings, hadn't he?'

The cub nodded.

'And that cat had a white tip to his tail, yes?'

'Yes.'

'The piece of tail your parents have is entirely black, isn't it?'

'Yes.'

'Then they are hunting the wrong cat, aren't they?'

'Yes,' came the soft reply.

'Why didn't you explain that to your parents?'

'I couldn't. I was knocked out. They left thinking I was dead.'

'What about you?' I asked the stronger one. 'You must have seen the cat who nearly killed your brother.'

He didn't answer. He stared at the ground sullenly and pretended to examine something intently.

'He couldn't tell them because he ran away,' said the smaller cub.

'I was ashamed,' the other one said.

'And now the other cat, who's probably the Shadow that everyone is so afraid of, is still out there while you're here on your own. Have you thought of that?'

Four eyes widened. They stared at me in horror. Obviously they hadn't thought of that.

14

All Aboard

I had to think quickly. How was I to get word back to the house? The tribe of sparrows could probably do that. Somehow the cubs would have to be taken to their parents. We had to show the foxes that both their cubs were alive, and we had to get them to listen to the truth. We could forget about the Shadow. Cat was right, he was long gone by now.

The small cub didn't look strong enough to make the journey without help. Dog was the only available means of transport. I had to get word to him, and quickly.

I explained to the sparrows what I needed them to do. They were delighted to accept the challenge. I told them that it might be dangerous, but, in truth, I didn't think it would be as long as they stayed away from the foxes. Everyone likes a little danger and the tribe was no different. They whooped and hollered among themselves and then, wheeling away in a cloud of beating wings, they flew off in their crazy formations.

A silence descended on the little clearing where the foxes had made their home. I was alone with the two cubs and suddenly I felt very vulnerable.

'Do you really think the bad cat is out there?' a little voice asked. I wasn't the only one feeling vulnerable.

'Do you know how to hide?'

They nodded enthusiastically.

'Well, go and hide. Don't come out until you hear me whistle, like this, see?' I gave them my best tune, the one that Mouse always likes.

'Got that, have you?'

More nodding of heads.

'Well, go hide then.'

In moments they had disappeared.

Now all I could do was wait.

It seemed like hours before Dog came lumbering into view. I've never been so pleased to see anyone as I was to see Dog at that moment. But I wasn't so greatly pleased to see Mouse clinging to the leather collar around Dog's neck. That was going to complicate the matter of transporting the cubs back to the house.

Dog saw me and started swishing his tail back and forth like a mad thing. 'Ha, Budgie, you survived!'

Mouse uncurled his tail from around Dog's ear. I never realised before how many animals had such long and useful tails. It occurred to me that Cat would miss hers badly.

'I'm so glad to see you, Dog,' I said.

'Same here,' Dog replied. 'If I have to hear another one of Mouse's songs, I will not be responsible for any accidental event involving a big bang on his head.'

'What's the matter with my songs?' Mouse protested, and before we could stop him, he burst into song.

'Don't go into the fox's den
Especially not at night.
And don't go in if you're a hen
Unless you learn to fight.

Don't go into the fox's lair
Specially during the day.
And don't go in if you're a hare
You'll never get away.

Don't go into the fox's house
Specially in the morning.
And don't go in if you're a mouse
Listen to my warning.'

'You see what I've had to put with?' grumbled Dog. 'And that wasn't the worst one either.'

'Ah, stop being an old grouch, Dog. You know you love it,' Mouse said, and then turning to me, he smiled broadly, holding his little arms aloft. 'Knew you could do it, Budgie. Didn't I say so, Dog? "If anyone can do it, Budgie can," I said. So what's the plan now, Budgie?'

I smiled to myself. Mouse's enthusiasm was infectious. 'It's not over yet. We've things to do,' I said and I explained the problem and what I intended to do.

I whistled my little tune, hoping the cubs would hear it. I didn't know how far they had gone to hide. I needn't have worried. Within seconds they were both in the clearing staring up with open mouths at Dog. I hoped it wasn't Mouse they had eyes for. He would make the perfect dinner for these guys.

Dog nodded and looked at the pups. 'Who's the oldest?' he asked.

'I am,' the bigger cub answered.

'You did your best for your little brother, didn't you?'

'Yes, I did,' the cub said without any conviction.

'I know you did.' Dog sighed. 'I'm sure you did. You know, I knew a fellow once and the exact same thing happened to him. Well, exact, except for one thing. You still have your brother. He doesn't.'

I had no idea what Dog was talking about. His head was down, and he was mumbling to himself. Something about little brothers and responsibilities. He was making no sense. It was sometime later that I discovered what all the mumblings were about but I had no time to worry about them now.

'What do you think, Dog? Will it be possible to get these fellows back to the house on your back?' I was looking at Mouse, wondering if he realised the danger of having two cubs as fellow passengers. But Mouse wasn't in the least put out.

'Course he can, big strong fellow like Dog. Plenty of room up here. Now then, young fellows, can you jump?'

'Are you sure, Mouse? You're not afraid of … you know … lunch and dinner business?'

'Nothing to fear. A mouse like me is made of two parts strychnine to one part nettles. One eency bitty taste of me and you will die like a crazy bluebottle. You wouldn't like that now, boys, would you?'

The two cubs shook their heads vigorously.

Mouse winked at me.

The cubs jumped onto Dog's back and we started our journey home.

The only way Dog could get across the river was to use the broken tree that lay to the east. The house was directly to the south. We were going to lose time.

'You should fly straight to the house,' Dog said. 'We left the sparrows looking after Cat but quite honestly they're a bit flaky and I didn't like the mood Cat was in when we left. She kept talking about facing up to the foxes. She said she could explain everything to them.'

'And just as we left, I saw the foxes at the pond,' Mouse added. 'They didn't look like the listening kind.'

'No,' said the two cubs together, 'they're not.'

I didn't know what I could do, but patience, I was discovering, was not my best quality. I had already wasted time waiting for Dog to arrive; now I was anxious to be away and find out what was happening.

I headed directly for the house. Dog and his crew on board would make it as soon as they could.

When I reached the garden, I could see the foxes.

And Cat.

She was clinging to a windowsill, snarling and screeching for all she was worth. The foxes had her cornered. She had nowhere to go. Foolish Cat. Why couldn't she have stayed indoors? One of the foxes held the piece of tail in the air. I could hear them yelling, 'This is yours. We can see it's yours. You're the one alright. Don't try to deny it.'

No, definitely not the listening kind.

Then I heard a flurry in the trees. The sparrows were there

looking at the scene unfolding beneath them. They started whistling and making noises. I supposed they were trying to distract the foxes. That won't work, I thought. Then they began screaming more loudly.

They were looking across to me, flapping their wings and pointing at something.

Then I saw a shadow spread across the lawn under me. Another shadow, I thought. Do they ever end?

I looked up. Too late. An ugly black hooded crow was diving straight at me. He had a look in his angry eyes of someone who would slice you open with his razor-sharp claws if you as much as flew across his shadow.

Thanks to the sparrows' warning I had just enough time to dip a fraction and roll away to one side, but he still clipped me on one wing, and I lost control. I flapped frantically, trying to regain my balance, but I plunged from the sky.

This time I knew there would be no soft Cat to land on.

I closed my eyes and waited.

15

A Fishy Business

I learnt later that when I hit the pond, I narrowly missed the fountain. Instead, I landed in the deepest part.

The water hit me like a stone, and then I sank into the darkness. The fall had knocked the air from my lungs. I couldn't move a muscle. I was alive, but my feet were entangled in green slimy weeds that were pulling me deeper into the pond. It was becoming harder to breathe and I was getting cold, drifting into unconsciousness, into a deep sleep. I was beginning to feel happy about letting go. If I did, everything would be all right. I wanted everything to be all right.

Then, from nowhere, I felt a punch in my ribcage. Then another, slapping into my back. Two goldfish slotted themselves under each of my wings, while two more pushed me upwards. The water became brighter. I could see sunlight. And goldfish. Hundreds of them. It seemed like all the goldfish in the pond were spread out before me. I was pushed through that golden cloud of fish and headed upwards.

The goldfish that we passed gathered in formations under me and just when I broke the surface they charged, all at once, pushing me from behind in a tremendous surge. I landed with a splash on the flowerbed beside the pond. The fish had chosen a soft place for my landing. I lay there among the flowers, coughing and wheezing. I've always hated water. Now I knew why.

It was a while before I was able compose myself and find out what was happening.

It seemed little had changed since my fall from the heavens except that everyone was staring at me, all of them frozen on the spot.

Cat was still clinging to the windowsill, but she wasn't snarling now. She was looking at me with her mouth gaping open. Even on Cat it wasn't an attractive look.

The foxes, too, were standing rigid, their backs arched in surprise. Of course, they had never seen me before, and they didn't know what to make of me. I must have looked a sight. I was covered in mud and trails of green pondweed hung from my head like a mouldy wig.

Cat was the first to recover.

She sprang from the windowsill and tried to escape, leaping high over a bed of long pampas grass and ferns. The foxes roared in anger and, forgetting about the strange apparition by the pond, charged after her.

But their chase came to a screeching halt and they fell to the ground, rolling over and screaming in pain, using a language I had never heard before.

Cat turned and smiled.

From the long grass a familiar head raised itself.

Hedgehog!

'Watch where you're going, you crazy people. Always in a rush nowadays. Slow down, why don't you? You could have injured me.'

The foxes lay there, groaning and trying to pick Hedgehog's thorny spikes from their feet. They had both stepped on him and he had rolled into a little ball of sharp needles. I did say he was a prickly customer.

I heard barking. Dog had made it home.

The cubs leapt from his back and ran to their parents.

Mouse came to inspect me. 'You look a sight, Budgie. I knew it was a bad idea to let you out on your own. I said so, Dog. Didn't I?'

But Dog wasn't listening. He had something to say to the foxes.

'Listen to your children for a change. They have something important to tell you.'

The cubs blurted out their story, interrupting each other and talking at the same time about white tails and river logs and being scared. Cat added a few comments to back up their story. The foxes didn't look convinced, but when the little cub Cat had saved went over to her and put his paw in hers, I think they realised the truth.

'Maybe the Shadow isn't a cat at all,' I said to them. They looked at me as if I had two heads. 'He could be a crow like the one who attacked me, or a hawk, maybe.'

'One thing's for sure, buddy,' said Hedgehog, 'he's definitely not you. Not all dressed up like that anyway.'

They all laughed.

I tried to take the green weeds out of my feathers, but I had to laugh too. Mouse in particular was enjoying the joke, pointing at me and crying, 'Would you look at that wig!'

Even Cat joined in. 'What a day this is. Budgie in a wig!'

The foxes left after saying sorry and thank you. They promised to visit if they ever got the chance.

The field mice who had been hiding in the house sensed that the foxes had gone and now the garden was swarming with the little things. They were leaving the house in droves, carrying all manner of items, from broken matchsticks to little metal screws. One even had a piece of green cheese on his back.

'Hey, you there, put that back! That's mine,' yelled Mouse. 'You can't have that. Flaming cheek! Put it down.'

Mouse ran after them, leaping about in a little rage that was bound to get him nowhere.

Dog funbilicated in that garumphous way he has. Everyone thought that Cat actually smiled. The goldfish clapped their fins and slapped the water in delight and the sparrows wheeled about in glorious circles. Hedgehog jumped with glee.

We all laughed in our own peculiar way.

What a day indeed!

Budgie's Notes

Dear reader,

I tried my hardest to make sure that no animals of any kind would be harmed in the writing of these annals. I regret to inform the reader that the writer (me) suffered some serious pain. I fell from the cage. I fell from a tree. And I fell from the sky.

When I describe it like that you must think that I'm a very clumsy bird. In my defence, I was pushed out of my cage when I wasn't ready. OK, I admit a bunch of sparrows shouldn't have frightened me out of a tree, but falling from the sky was not my fault. I was attacked by a crow.

I recovered, as did Cat. She lost a bit of her tail, but it healed nicely. It didn't affect her attitude. She still swept into our living room as if she owned the place and she still waved her tail as if it was as long as it once was.

The fox cubs have also recovered and, as it is with all these youngsters, will probably not remember anything about the events of that day.

The goldfish have memories as long as a cat's tail and they will never forget that I plunged into their pool-causing a minor tsunami which churned their little world a bit. I'll never forget that either. They saved my life, and for that I will always be grateful to them.

A group of sparrows is in fact called a tribe. Being a member of their family made me feel so proud and special. Belonging to a group of similar beings is a basic tool of survival. We can achieve more if there are more of us. We learn from each other faster. Just think of the names we have for groups of animals. A herd of cows, a flock of sheep, a shoal of fish, a colony of bats, a swarm of bees, a caravan of camels, a tower of giraffes, a congregation of alligators and a pod of whales, to name a few.

A flock of budgies is known as a chatter. A lone bird like me in a cage doesn't have a title. I'm just a budgie. I think I miss the chatter. I was singled out that day by a hooded crow because I was on my own. Luckily for me, the crow was also on his own. A group of crows are known as a murder of crows. Gives me the shivers just to think about it. A murder of crows.

The Shadow hasn't been spotted in our area since. We all suspect that he's still out there and it's just a matter of time before he turns up. Of course, we have long discussions about who he could be. Some of us are certain that it must have been Cat's boyfriend. Others thought it may have been that hooded crow who nearly killed me.

Before you go, I should tell you that some of the words you read in this story can't be found in any dictionary.

I made them up.
Please forgive me.
Budgie.

BOOK TWO

One Eye

Contents

1

Murder

Such a brutal and terrible word.

Murder.

I never thought that I could become involved in such a thing.

And yet that's what it was.

Murder.

Cat's not bothered. Killing is second nature to her.

Mouse shrugs. He's not concerned either.

And Dog says, 'Sometimes you have to accept things, Budgie. Let it go. It's for the best.'

Dog, of course, is always right, but I can't just let it go as if it had never happened. It's in my head. It won't go away.

As you know, I'm a bird. And you probably know that I've been told many times that I'm a really lovely green and yellow bird. I'm a parrot but they keep calling me a budgie. Never mind. I have loads of friends, even though I'm in this cage.

The fact is, I'm not supposed to murder people.

I didn't actually commit murder. I'm too small. But my decision was what caused it.

I have to tell my story while it's fresh in my mind. Maybe that will ease my conscience. I hope so.

It all started not long after the Shadow affair.

Everyone in the house was relaxed. No problems to be resolved. We had settled into our routines. Thanks to Mouse, I had learnt to escape from the cage on my own and get out into the garden. I liked my days out, practising my flying skills and talking to old friends, like the goldfish and of course the sparrows. They were happy days. No shadows in the garden.

Then one day Mouse, as was his custom, was sitting in the corner of my cage, greedily chewing my seeds. He spat out the husks, not caring if they landed in the cage or spilled over onto the floor below. Something was on his mind.

'Do you hear anything strange during the night, Budgie?' he asked.

'Strange? I don't think so, no,' I said.

In truth, I thought the question was amusing. The only strange sounds Mouse was likely to hear were the rumblings of his own stomach, which were constantly making themselves heard, except, of course, when he was chewing on something with his sharp little teeth. Nothing could be heard above that. It was like listening to a drill.

He continued thoughtfully chewing on my seeds. The drill was switched to masonry mode and was grinding horribly. 'Well, I'm hearing things and I'm telling you, Budgie, I'm feeling things too. Something's going on. I don't know what it is, but I don't like it.'

'There must be a simple explanation,' I said. 'Have you asked the others?'

'No. Cat's away again and Dog is always asleep these days. Maybe you could make some enquiries among your friends when you're out and about.'

I promised that I would.

We said goodbye and I didn't give it any more serious thought.

That night, I needed my sleep. I had been out all day and my wings were feeling the pain. I have a habit of overdoing things. I must take more care of myself. Mouse stayed the night and snored his little head off, but eventually I was able to get to sleep. I had no doubt that Mouse wouldn't hear anything that night. I certainly didn't, not even the growling sounds coming from his stomach.

The next morning when I awoke, Mouse had gone.

That wasn't unusual. Mouse was an early riser. The seed dish was empty, so he was no doubt scavenging in the kitchen for his breakfast. I opened the cage door. I was now an expert at unlocking the door. I sometimes felt that I'd make a good burglar, but then again, the only practice I got was breaking out. Burglars had to break in. I thought that might require a different skill set. Little did I know then that I would be using that skill for a crime that would haunt me for a long time.

I decided to ask Dog about Mouse's strange sounds. When I found him, he was in the garden staring morosely at the pond.

'Good morning, Dog,' I greeted him in my best cheerful early-morning voice.

He looked at me with baleful eyes. 'Ah, Budgie, there you are,' he said. 'Is it?'

This was not like Dog at all.

'Of course it is,' I replied. 'Look around. The sun is up. The flowers are blooming. All sorts of birds, flying about and singing. Ah, look over there! My friends the sparrows are practising one of their flying formation dances. What a sight.'

But Dog remained unmoved.

'What's the matter, Dog?'

'You haven't heard the news then,' Dog said. 'We're getting a new resident.'

'No, I haven't heard that. What sort of resident?'

'Another dog, like me.'

So that was it, I thought. Dog was jealous. Maybe a little bit afraid too. He wouldn't be the only dog in the house any more. Maybe not even the top dog.

'Like you?' I asked.

'Well, like me but younger, a lot younger. Just a little pup really. Different colour too. Golden hair. Supposed to be very handsome if you like your dogs yellow.'

'What's the problem? A young pup will give you something to do. You'll be able to teach him things. He'll be like the son you never had. There's no need to be down in the dumps.'

'Yes, I know. It might turn out for the best, but I can't help feeling that he's to be my replacement. I'm not getting any younger. I was at the vet's last week and there was talk about me that I couldn't understand. Something about Cat's tracks, though what that has to do with me, I don't know. That's when the question of the new pup arose. Budgie, the fact is, I think I may be going to die soon. My eyesight is fading and I'm afraid …' Dog choked back a tear.

I wasn't expecting that, I can tell you. I couldn't imagine

the house without Dog. Surely it wasn't possible. I didn't know what to say.

'I hadn't thought about what you said though,' Dog continued, pulling himself together. 'Taking him under my wing, as it were, and teaching him things.' Dog laughed for the first time. 'Did you hear what I said, Budgie? Taking him under my wing. Ha! I suppose he wouldn't fit under your wing. Ha! As if I had a wing.'

It was a relief to hear Dog laugh. But suddenly his mood swung back the other way.

'I had a little brother once,' he said. He hesitated for a moment and then began talking to himself as if I wasn't there. 'He was a good little lad, but I failed him. This is another chance. I mustn't fail this little pup.'

He wandered off in the direction of the pond. I was so worried about him that I completely forgot to ask about Mouse's strange noises in the night.

2

Pup

The next day I was dozing in my cage, minding my own business, when I heard a scraping noise in the seed dish.

'Mouse,' I whispered. I have no idea why I whispered. There was no one else in the room. 'Is that you?'

'Stop squawking,' Mouse complained.

I noticed that he didn't keep his voice down. Oh no! Typical Mouse! Sometimes he could be completely irrational.

'I'm not squawking.' Again, I found myself whispering. Why do I do that? 'Why shouldn't I squawk anyway? There's no one around to hear me.'

'I've something on my mind,' he announced grimly.

He wouldn't say anything until he had his mouth stuffed with seeds. 'Ah, fat's much feffer. I needed fat. I've been forking rather fard.'

He went on munching and grinding until finally he'd

satisfied himself and we could manage a normal conversation.

'As I was saying,' he said, 'I've been working very hard. I've examined all my little passageways and made repairs where necessary. There's a lot to do. Those little field mice that got in a while ago destroyed more than I thought.'

'But why? Are you afraid of something?'

'That I am, Budgie, that I am.' And with that he stuffed his mouth with seeds again. I think I've forgotten what a seed tastes like. I never get any.

'Have you heard the news about a new pup coming to live with us?' I asked. 'Dog is not best pleased about it.'

'Not only heard, Budgie, I've seen the little blighter. He arrived not ten minutes ago, bawling his eyes out. Amazed you didn't hear him. Is there something wrong with your hearing?'

The news of the pup's arrival surprised me. I must have dozed off for longer than I thought.

'Anyway, he's out there in the kitchen. He's been given a little wooden box for himself, but now he's kicking and biting anything he can get his teeth into,' Mouse continued. 'Looks like he's going to be a real handful. Poor Dog, getting stuck with a little monster like that. By the way, I've been meaning to ask, is there any news of Cat? I really wish she was here.'

You could have blown me over with a sparrow's tail feather. I was shocked. Mouse, of all people, hoping for Cat to come back. I knew he was always careful not to get too close to her. He was forever telling me to be on my guard. 'Never trust her an inch,' he'd say. 'You just never can tell with cats.' That was his motto and he never stopped drumming it into me. 'One swipe,' he'd warn me, 'and you're a goner. Sure as anything.'

And now he couldn't wait for her to come home! Our little world was certainly shifting in mysterious ways and no mistake. I didn't know what to make of it.

'Let's go and meet this little pup,' I said. 'We'll talk about Cat later.'

We went into the kitchen. In the corner next to Dog's bed there was a small wooden box. This was new. There was fresh straw and an old blanket in it, but there was no one there. I flew into the box and snuffled around. I saw a disgusting pink bone that had been well chewed, and an old carpet slipper that had also seen better days.

'All clear?' shouted Mouse.

'Yes, but I don't see the pup. Are you sure he's here?'

Suddenly before I could say 'nudge' I saw a little dog racing towards the box. And before I could warn Mouse, I realised that the little thing wasn't intent on friendly greetings.

By any standards, he was very beautiful – long golden locks, glistening and rippling as he bounded towards us. I looked at him. His eyes were glazed over as if he were somewhere else.

'Robbers,' he shouted. 'Get away from my things. They're mine.'

I've described him as little, and he was, by dog standards, that is. Compared to me and Mouse he was huge. He barked. A little frightened croak of a bark. He was doing his best to make himself look bigger and more dangerous, which was unnecessary. I had no doubt that if he charged into me or Mouse neither of us would survive the blow.

I flew out of reach, shouting my warning to Mouse, or 'squawking' as he would no doubt describe it. I needn't have feared for him though. He deftly stepped to one side. Pup swerved and lost his footing. He slid along the tiled floor, missed his box and crashed into the wall. He lay there stunned.

Mouse stepped out from behind the leg of a chair. 'Olé,' he shouted.

I started to giggle, which set Mouse off. I suppose that wasn't very nice of us, but sometimes you just have to laugh.

Pup didn't see the funny side, though. He lay there, snarling and baring his teeth like dogs do.

I became concerned. Not for the pup's health – he was just winded. I was worried that he'd soon be on his feet again, and we'd have to be extra careful. A wounded animal is unpredictable.

'Who are you?' he panted, 'and why are you stealing my things?'

I explained who we were and pointed out that little fellows like us wouldn't be able to lift any of his things, never mind steal them. 'And we're friends of Dog,' I added, thinking that would satisfy him.

It didn't. It only plunged him into an even worse humour.

'Dog!' He spat it out as if it was a bad word. 'That big lump of a smelly old thing. He's useless. He said he was going to take me under his wing. He thought that was very funny. I don't want to go under his wing, wherever that is. I want to stay here with my friend.'

'You have a friend?' asked Mouse, peering at Pup with interest. 'Does he live around here?'

Pup snorted. 'He does now. He came with me from the last place. That was an awful place. Bad things happened there. My friend had to get out so he stayed with me.'

'Where is he now?' Mouse asked, anxiously looking over his shoulder.

From my vantage point I could see no one else in the kitchen. 'All clear, Mouse,' I said.

Relieved, Mouse asked again, 'Where is he now and what does he look like?'

'Out looking for a place to live, I suppose,' Pup said. 'But he'll be back soon, and he'll make mincemeat of both of you. He's bigger than you and he has big teeth. He has only one eye though. Lost the other one in a fight. But he can still see things even I can't see. I'm going to tell him about you. When you see him you'll be scared.'

Pup got to his feet.

I was already scared. 'Come on, Mouse. Let's go.'

'What's his name?' asked Mouse.

Pup was on his feet and shaking himself. He had that look in his eyes again.

'He's a rat,' Pup said. 'They call him One Eye.'

3

Mouseworld

'I knew it. I knew it. I told you, Budgie, didn't I? I told you. A rat. That's bad news, Budgie, really bad news.'

Mouse was agitated, checking this way and that before he crossed an open space and looking carefully around a corner before putting a foot forward. I decided not to tell him that whatever he had told me, he had made no mention of a rat. Of that I was certain.

'I told you, didn't I? I said we needed Cat here. I told you.'

So that was why he wanted Cat home again. To a certain extent I was relieved. Mouse wasn't going crazy after all. For him it was a case of the lesser of two evils. Cat could be a threat but since the Shadow affair there was a truce between the two. He still didn't entirely trust her, but she was better than a rat. A rat would kill Mouse just for pleasure.

'A rat, of all things,' he mumbled. 'And I'll tell you this, Budgie, where there's one there are always two. Where there are two there's sure to be more. We'll be overrun in no time.'

I found out later that a group of rats was called a mischief of rats. Sounds almost playful, not like a murder of crows. I still shudder about that one. 'I wonder if they'll all have one eye,' I said.

Mouse stopped in his tracks. 'That's another thing. I definitely do not like the sound of this one-eye business. They say if you lose one of your senses like sight or hearing your other senses get stronger. Sounds like this rat has developed a super eye to compensate for the loss of his other one. Evolution, that's what it's called.'

'It's not really the same thing though, is it?' I said. 'How could a super eye evolve so quickly? And Pup saying that the rat can see things that he can't see doesn't mean much. He's just a pup, after all, and anyway, how dangerous can just one eye be to us even if it is a super eye? What's a super eye anyway?'

I didn't see any reason to worry about a one-eyed rat in a house with a big brute of a dog and a natural born hunter like Cat.

But Mouse shook his head. 'Perhaps, but I don't like all these questions,' he said.

We soon found out that Mouse was absolutely right to be frightened of the rat's eye.

'Come, Budgie, it's time you visited my little kingdom while it's still mine.'

He pulled back a small mat that lay under a side table.

In every wooden floor you will find knots where branches had once grown out of the main trunk of the tree. Mouse pushed down on one of these knots. After a grunt or two, the knot fell inwards and a hole, large enough for a little mouse to squeeze through, appeared in the floor.

'Are you coming in?' Mouse asked.

I looked into the opening and hesitated. It was dark in the hole. 'I won't be able to see a thing down there,' I protested. I didn't like to say that I was quite frightened of the dark. I wasn't built for flying at night like some owl or bat. I wasn't built to go underground either.

Mouse waved my worries away. 'Don't worry about that. I've invented a lighting system. Simple but genius even if I say so myself. You'll be OK, Budgie,' he assured me.

And that's why I went into the hole.

Mad, you say.

Me too.

But nothing ventured, nothing gained. Remind me to wipe that phrase from my vocabulary.

The space I found myself in was surprisingly large and airy. It was very dark, but my eyes gradually adjusted so that I could make out the walls. Further in, I could see nothing at all, just blackness stretching out forever.

'Is this where you live?' I asked Mouse.

'No, not here. This is just the space under the living room. There are many spaces like this under the house, but they're cold and miserable, and as you can see, black as the soul of a rat.'

'What about your lighting system?'

'Follow me, Budgie. Just up here. Watch your step.'

We climbed upwards on narrow plastic steps. There was something familiar about them. I looked more closely. I was sure they were purple. 'Mouse, you devil,' I yelled. 'This is the ladder from my cage. You stole it. I wondered what had happened to it.'

'Ah, Budgie, you didn't miss it, did you?'

I had to laugh. What a rogue Mouse was!

We reached the next level and stepped into a long corridor. It was bright and I could see more easily. We were behind one of the living room walls.

Little rays of light streamed in from tiny holes punched randomly in the wall. Mouse had placed small pieces of a broken mirror in places where they would catch the rays and send them in different directions around the corridor, lighting up the whole space.

'Ingenious, isn't it?' Mouse said proudly. 'You might think that I just punched a few holes here and there, but it's all been done according to a very careful plan. I had to select the spots for the holes from the outside because they had to be concealed in the wallpaper pattern so that nobody would be able to see them. That's why I needed the ladder. Some places I just couldn't reach without it. I have plans to go higher when I get the time. Maybe that could be a job for you, Budgie, seeing as how you can fly and all. That's a good idea. Don't know why I didn't think of that before.'

I had to give credit to Mouse. He had certainly made himself an interesting home. We wandered down seemingly endless corridors, a vast world of hidden nooks and crannies with secret hiding places behind the walls of every room in the house.

Mouse showed me where he stored emergency supplies for every eventuality. He even had an old toy steamship – 'In case we're flooded,' he explained – but I don't think he was serious. I'm sure the boat would sink without a trace. I could see holes in the hull bigger than the one in the floorboards where we had crawled into Mouse's world.

The thought of that hole suddenly sent a shiver of panic through me. Where were we? We had come so far into this labyrinth that I had no idea where we were. The thought of being trapped underground filled me with fear.

'I hope you know the way out of here, Mouse,' I said, but before he could answer we heard a low grunt.

'What's that?'

'Shh,' Mouse whispered. Definitely a whisper now.

I stayed quite still.

Mouse was being, as you'd expect, as quiet as a mouse.

The grunting started up again and then we heard a tearing, crunching sound. Suddenly a sharp burst of bright light came flooding into the corridor. A large nose snuffled into view. Then an eye was looking at us.

A big, gleaming, evil eye.

4

The Eye

'Run, Budgie, run!' Mouse screamed at me. 'It's the rat.'

Mouse had been leading the way. Now, suddenly, I had to turn around and run while he kept prodding me in the rear, shouting, 'Hurry up! Go faster, why don't you!'

Now, I'll admit I'm not really very good on my feet. Firstly, I've only two, while Mouse has four. He was always going to be faster than me, but in the cramped and narrow passageways of Mouse's world, he wasn't able to get past me.

And then, as if things weren't bad enough, we birds must hop along using two feet at the same time. The problem was that the ceiling in places was so low that I kept bumping my head against it. Between that and Mouse's roaring, I was developing a ferocious headache.

'Turn right here,' Mouse would say. 'Now, a sharp left and then straight on. No! Straight on. Here, yes. Hurry up!'

This went on for some time. My head wouldn't take much more banging. Nothing ventured, indeed.

'Stop!' Mouse yelled.

We stopped.

There was an opening in the wall and a pinpoint of light was streaming in.

'I can't hear a thing, can you?'

I listened. Mouse was right. Wherever the rat had got to, he wasn't chasing us from behind.

'I'm going to take a peek from up here,' Mouse said. He yanked on some sort of pulley and the stream of light grew wider. A hole that was big enough for him to get through opened up. He climbed into it and vanished.

'Don't leave me here, Mouse,' I yelled.

I don't mind admitting that I was terrified. Can you imagine? There I was alone in the dark, in a strange place, probably underground, with just a little shaft of light to tell me where I was.

I thought of all my canary relatives who, years ago, were brought down into the dark coal mines and kept in cages, miles underground, to act as a warning of gas leaks. If the canaries died, that meant there was lethal gas in the shafts, and the miners would know they had to get out. It was definitely all over when the canary stopped singing!

Mouse popped his head back into the opening.

'Don't be silly, I'm not leaving you. Get up here and have a look. It's the rat, all right, and he's huge. And stop that singing.'

I wasn't aware that I'd been singing. Strange how the mind works. I must have thought I was the canary in the mine, trying to keep us alive. Maybe I need a psychiatrist.

With difficulty, I crawled through the hole. Mouse was perched on a ledge high up in the living room. I was relieved to see my cage standing in the corner. At last I was out of Mouseworld. I didn't care to go back there again.

'Don't make any sudden moves,' Mouse hissed.

The ledge we were standing on turned out to be the top of a picture frame. I knew the picture. I could see it from my cage. Irony of ironies. It was a painting of miners in a dark cavern, glistening with sweat and struggling to push a large, wheeled bucket full of coal along railway tracks. They wore helmets with shining lamps that lit up the picture. There were no canaries to be seen.

'See over there,' Mouse whispered. He pointed to our right, and I saw the rat.

He was halfway through the wall, gnawing at the wood and the wallpaper, trying to get into Mouseworld. I could only see half of him, but he was certainly big. At least five times the size of Mouse, and heavy with it. He was black, with a long hairless tail that cracked on the wooden floorboards like a loathsome leather whip. I couldn't see his face, which was buried in the wall, but it wouldn't be long before I was to have that dubious pleasure.

'You think that's One Eye?' I asked.

'Has to be him,' Mouse replied. 'He's after me for sure, but he'll never get me. I can hide out in my little caves. He'll never find me. You can always fly to your cage and lock yourself in. The fact remains, though, we'll have to get rid of him somehow. But he's so big. Look at the size of him. Cat could take him out, I'm sure, but even she might struggle.'

Suddenly the rat stopped his work and slowly withdrew from the wall. His two ears perked up. They were torn in places and looked like a pair of old rags flapping about in the wind. Except there was no wind in the living room. I guessed that his ears were very sensitive, more compensation for the eye he'd lost.

I was right.

'Ah, little voices I can hear,' the rat said. 'Whispering, are you?' He spoke in a low rusty voice, rasping and growling.

Now we could see his full size. He was enormous. His most striking feature was the eye. It was big. It was double the size you would expect in a rat's head. The remains of his other eye had long grown over and disappeared. I had never seen anything like it. A one-eyed monster.

The eye scanned the room and within seconds focused on us. We shuffled back, nervous but not scared yet. Unless the rat could jump twenty times his height, we'd be safe.

'I spy with my big eye something beginning with D,' he said. 'And if I'm not mistaken, you must be Mouse, which means that you, in the colourful pyjamas, must be Budgie. Great little gigglers, I hear.'

So Pup had been talking to him.

One Eye scuttled closer to us across the floor, his claws scratching the wood as if he were using it to sharpen them. You could feel and hear his weight, dripping with menace, as he flexed his muscles and raised his eye to look at us.

'You don't know me,' he said, matter-of-factly, 'but I'm going to kill you. Very soon.'

5

D Is for Dinner

It was very strange to hear a rat laugh. Normally they
don't, which is just as well, because a rat's laugh could
turn your blood ice cold.

'I spy with my big eye something beginning with D,' the
rat said again, slower this time. '*D* is for dinner,' he chuckled,
'and you're it.'

I couldn't see how he was going to get to us. Surely, he
wasn't able to fly.

I looked longingly across the room at my cage. I would
have given anything to be tucked up in my bed at that
moment, secure behind the bars of my home. Just one little
glide and I'd be there.

'Don't think about it,' Mouse said. 'Now that I see him,
I reckon that big fellow down there could topple your cage
in an instant. You'd be trapped, unable to get out and on the
floor, exactly where he wants you. He'd break into the cage.

You'd be dinner, all right, Budgie.'

I looked at Rat again. Mouse was right. He'd have no trouble pulling down my cage. He was enormous.

'Don't you worry, Mouse, I wouldn't leave you on your own.' I felt a little ashamed that I had just been thinking about doing just that. I wondered, not for the first time, how the little rascal seemed able to read my mind.

'But where else can I go?' I asked. 'I can't live with you in those dungeons. I'm not equipped to live underground. Maybe I should just go down and talk to One Eye. He seems like a reasonable fellow.'

Mouse turned and hissed at me angrily.

'What are you saying, Budgie?' he yelled. 'Tell me, what is it that you can see down there?'

'Why, the big rat, of course,' I replied.

'Have you noticed anything? Has he changed at all?'

'Well, now you mention it, that eye of his is a lot bigger. Getting bigger all the time. Is that a bad thing? It's funny, but I'm beginning to feel good about it. What a wonderful eye it is, don't you think? There's a light shining from it that's glowing in blue mist. I feel like I'm floating on a warm, gentle cloud. There's nothing to be afraid of. I'm sliding down into the clouds.'

Suddenly, I wanted to fly down and talk to the rat but Mouse put a stop to that.

'Don't look into his eye, Budgie. He's trying to take you over. Just close your eyes and stay where you are. I have a plan.'

Mouse twitched his tail. He stood up on his hind legs and stroked his whiskers. I could tell that he was about to do something horrendously stupid. Mouse isn't usually stupid but at times he can be rash. He tends to do things that not only put his own life in danger but also the life of anyone who might be standing next to him.

That's what concerned me.

I was standing next to him.

There I was, clinging to a precarious ledge and, given my history of falling from heights, it is fair to say that I was getting quite anxious. Also, it's difficult to maintain your balance when you have your eyes closed. Try it sometime, you'll see I'm right.

'Mouse,' I whispered. I admit that this time maybe I squawked. 'Please stop. Please don't upset him. We can go down and talk to him. Please.'

But Mouse wasn't listening. He was on a roll and couldn't be stopped. I heard him belching and heaving and slurping his tongue around his mouth.

'Don't do it, Mouse,' I yelled.

But it was too late. Mouse blew a stream of half chewed seeds, mixed with bile from his stomach, directly at Rat.

I've already said that Mouse was becoming increasingly accurate when he spat out seeds as if they were little bullets. This time the volley he let loose was more like a cannonball. All those congealed seeds flew through the air straight at One Eye. Whether by accident or design, Mouse's cannonball hit the rat squarely in the eye. What a shot!

One Eye fell to the ground, screaming terribly. Then I saw that his eye had suddenly shrunk to half the size it had been. The blue hue that had been so comforting to me disappeared in an instant.

'What's happened?' I asked. It was as if I had just awoken from a bad dream. 'Where are we?'

'Well, I don't know where you've been, Budgie, but it was nowhere nice. I don't think you should look into that rat's eye any longer. You were mesmerised by it.'

Some sort of magic, I thought.

'No, nothing like that. Magic is overrated. Must be a kind of hypnosis. I don't know about it but I'm going to find out. You were really in his power there until we broke his concentration.' There he was again, reading my thoughts.

The big rat beneath us was scraping Mouse's seeds from his eye and hurling terrible curses in our direction. We weren't giggling this time.

'I'm coming after you,' he screamed. 'Stay where you are. I'm coming after you.'

'Mouse, I think we should go.' I was getting nervous. I could feel myself wanting to look at that eye again. I didn't think I'd be able to resist, and once I looked into it, I wouldn't be able to look away again. Those calm blue colours were so gentle and yet so powerful that I had lost any will to resist. I couldn't believe that I had wanted to talk to that terrible creature. How could I have thought he was nice? I was firmly under the spell of that horrible eye and only for good old Mouse's missile of spit and seed, I would surely be dead by now. Mouse had broken the spell and I didn't want to go near that eye again.

'We're not going anywhere, Budgie. Let's see what he can do.'

I told you Mouse was reckless.

'But what about that eye? Can you not feel its power? Are you not afraid to look at it?'

'Doesn't seem to affect me,' Mouse replied. 'Maybe it's a mouse thing or maybe it's just a matter of willpower. Just close two of those six eyelids you're always telling me you have. How hard can that be? Oh look, here he comes.'

But I couldn't look. I closed all six of my eyelids.

'Tell me what's happening.'

'Nothing yet. He doesn't seem to have a plan. Oh wait, he's heading for your cage, Budgie. He's standing on his hind legs. Wow! He's big when you see him like that. Now he's huffing and pushing it. The cage doesn't stand a chance.'

I couldn't stop myself. I opened my eyes just in time to see my cage topple over with a crash. The door broke open and my seeds burst everywhere. Had I been in the cage, the rat would surely have captured me. From now on I had to stay in the air. I was glad I had learnt to fly all those weeks ago.

One Eye looked up at us, grinning viciously. I closed my eyes quickly.

'No more seeds for you, Mouse,' I heard him say. His voice sent a cold shudder through my bones. It was filled with menace. 'I'm going to deal with you two.'

'Oh, I don't think so, you big lug,' Mouse laughed.

I thought my friend had gone mad. Why was he goading the rat?

'What are you doing? Are you insane?' I asked him.

'Open your eyes, Budgie. Take a look at who's standing in the doorway.'

When I looked, my heart skipped several beats.

Standing in the doorway, looking at the rat with those familiar slanting, yellow eyes, was Cat.

And One Eye had seen her too.

6

A Close Shave

That night I slept outside in the garden. I couldn't use the cage any more. The house was unsafe for me and for Mouse, although he insisted on staying in Mouseworld. The events of the day had fairly worn me out.

Let me tell you what happened.

Cat was in danger, but she didn't know it yet. Neither did we.

Mouse and I were on the picture frame cheering and whistling for all we were worth, trying our best to give her every encouragement. 'Attack! Go for him, Cat,' we yelled.

One Eye stood his ground. So did Cat. Neither made a move.

'What's the matter, Cat?' Mouse shouted. 'You can take him. He's just a rat.'

Something was wrong. One Eye wasn't retreating. He looked determined. Cat wasn't moving either, but she looked as though she couldn't. She looked frozen to the spot.

'Oh no. Cat's looking into his eye. I bet he's putting her into a trance. Mouse, you've got to do something, and quickly.'

'But what can I do?' Mouse wailed. 'I've no more seeds to chuck at him. We'll have to think of something else.'

We shouted and jumped about, trying to break One Eye's concentration, but he was unmoved. His eye was focused squarely on Cat, who had now collapsed to the floor, a stupid grin spreading across her face. Any minute now and she would roll over. Then it would be a simple matter for One Eye to stroll up to her and sink his sharp teeth into her throat. We had to do something.

Then I had a brainwave.

'Mouse, I have an idea. But it's dangerous.'

'Does it involve me?' Mouse asked.

'No, just me.'

'Then go for it, Budgie. There's no time to lose. I'll stay here as back up.'

Just when I come up with a reckless and totally lunatic plan, Mouse goes all cautious on me.

I had noticed that my mirror, which you'll remember was made of magnifying glass, had rolled out of my cage and was lying on the floor behind Cat.

It was turned upside down and I couldn't see if the glass had shattered or if it was still intact. For my plan to work it had to be still intact.

Mouse saw what I was looking at and nodded. 'Good idea,' he said.

I launched myself off the ledge of the picture frame and

flew as quietly as I could, landing behind Cat. I was hoping One Eye wouldn't notice me. Bright yellow and green are not the best colours to take into battle. But I needn't have worried – One Eye was concentrating only on Cat. I made sure I didn't look into that eye, but it took all my willpower. I could feel its force even though it wasn't aimed at me.

I reached the mirror and turned it over. It was still intact, just a tiny crack down its middle. It would have to do.

I managed to tilt it on its side and slide it out from behind Cat into the open. I turned it towards the rat, holding it up and hiding myself behind it. I began shouting, 'Hey, One Eye. Look at me. Here I am.'

If my plan didn't work, I hoped Mouse would warn me to get out of there in time. I was too busy hiding with my eyes closed to know what was happening in front of the mirror.

Mouse told me later that One Eye looked into the mirror. He saw the reflection of his own eye magnified ten times and he froze. He couldn't tear his eye away from his own reflection. He looked dazed. He started grinning.

'We've got him,' Mouse roared. 'He's going under.'

'Shhh, don't distract him,' I said.

Cat was slowly recovering. One Eye had lost his grip on her. She got to her feet just as the rat was beginning to lose control of his own legs. He was stumbling about, trying to stay upright, but he was losing the battle.

'Kill him, Cat,' Mouse yelled with glee. 'Kill the one-eyed monster. That'll teach him a lesson not to poke his eye into our house, so it will.'

Victory was ours. Then disaster snatched it from our grasp in an instant.

Cat had recovered but just like me, she had no memory of what had happened. She saw me crouching behind the mirror and then she saw the rat. Her face creased in concern. 'Are you OK, Budgie?' she asked and swept the mirror away to see if I was all right.

The mirror broke along its hairline fracture and shattered into pieces. In that moment the spell was broken, and Rat shook himself free. He recovered faster than either Cat or I had, and he scuttled away at an alarming speed for a creature of his size.

We had survived but the enemy had escaped.

'Drat,' was all Mouse could say.

'What just happened to me?' asked Cat, her gaze taking in the wreckage of the sitting room. 'This place is in a mess,' she said needlessly.

We told her about the one-eyed rat and how close he came to killing her. She didn't remember a thing.

'We'll have to call a meeting,' I said. 'We have to explain to everyone about the power of that horrible eye and what it can do. Maybe someone will come up with a plan about how to deal with this fellow. I don't think he'll fall for the mirror trick again.'

'By the way, Budgie,' said Mouse, 'that was a great move of yours with the mirror. Glad you were able to learn something from my lighting system.'

I said nothing. Maybe he was right. Maybe, without thinking it, I had got my inspiration from his mad lighting system. But I still had to carry it through without any help from him. Just one word of praise was all he had to give me.

'Brilliant, Budgie. You were absolutely brilliant,' he said.

'And that's two words, by the way.'

How did he do that? How could he read my mind?

So now here I was, homeless and sleeping outdoors with the tribe of sparrows who, I might add, snored considerably louder than Mouse. When one stops, another two will start. Little faint whistling sounds that reach a crescendo and then collapse into softer waves. The sparrows snore in a way that resembles their flight formations.

I didn't think that I'd be able to sleep but I did.

Tomorrow we would have our meeting.

7

The Meeting

It was strange to be holding our meeting outdoors for the first time. Normally our meetings took place in the living room. I usually set the agenda and acted as chairman, although, as I may have mentioned before, our meetings don't always proceed as planned.

We had chosen a spot under a lilac tree beside the fishpond. Mouse and I took up positions in the lower branches. I admit I was a little uncomfortable about this. I thought my green and yellow plumage clashed terribly with the purple flowers of the tree, besides which, there was a host of colourful butterflies, who I'm told are particularly attracted to the lilac tree, flitting in and out of the branches all through the meeting. Butterflies, like most insects, are harmless of course and cannot understand a word we say but their wonderful vibrant colours made me feel positively dowdy. Still, I shouldn't be jealous, they don't have much of a life. A few weeks at most,

I believe. I only mention this because our own lives, at this point, might also be measured in weeks or even days if we couldn't find a solution to our rat problem.

I called the meeting to order. 'Lady and gentlemen,' I began. I always began our meetings that way, but this time I got no further.

'Ah, suck a seed, Budgie,' Mouse interrupted. 'No formalities. We know why we're here. How are we to get rid of One Eye? That's the question. Any answers?'

To my surprise, Cat answered. She hardly ever says anything at our meetings and this time her contribution was chilling.

'We have to kill him,' she said matter-of-factly. 'He's a pest.'

'Right,' Mouse said. 'Well put, Cat. But how? Dog, any ideas? By the way, have you met our little one-eyed monster yet?'

I didn't like the way Mouse was taking over the meeting. I was the chairman. Everyone knew that. No one had asked Dog about Pup. A good chairman knows when to intervene.

'Where's Pup, Dog?' I asked. 'If he's a resident, he's entitled to be here, that is, if he wants to be here.'

'He'll be here later,' said Dog. 'He has something to do first. I would like your permission, chairman, to address the meeting. I have a few things to say.'

'Go ahead,' Mouse and I said at the same time. I glared at him, but he ignored me.

'Well, I don't know where to begin really, but first I should answer your question, Mouse. No, I don't think I've met One Eye yet, but yes, maybe I have. Let me explain.' He paused to gather his thoughts. 'It's a long story. First, I know some of you have met Pup and I realise you don't think much of him. He hasn't made a good first impression, but I'm asking you to give him a chance. You, Budgie, and you, Cat, have both been under the spell of this rat we are calling One Eye. You know what happened to you. He was going to kill you and you were powerless to prevent it. But imagine if instead he kept you alive as a slave to do his evil work for him. Imagine you believed everything he said and everything he told you to do. You might even betray your own mother.

'Well, that's Pup's story. He is torn with guilt about his mother. Some time ago he brought her to an isolated spot on a made-up excuse that One Eye had programmed him to say. She had no chance on her own against the brute. The rat killed her. Why? I don't know yet, but I have my suspicions. We can learn something from that. Budgie, you were saved by Mouse. Is that not so?'

'Yes, absolutely,' I agreed.

'And you, Cat, you were saved by Budgie. Correct?'

'Indeed,' purred Cat. 'I owe Budgie one.'

I don't know whether Cat meant it or not but that didn't come out right. In fact, it made me shudder.

'I mean one of my nine lives, Budgie.'

'Oh,' I managed to say. I think she was playing with me. It's hard to tell with Cat.

Dog went on: 'Pup's mother, remember, was a dog. From the look of Pup, I'd say she wasn't much smaller than me, but One Eye was still able to kill her, more than likely because she was on her own. I don't think any one of us can resist whatever power he has in that eye, but it seems to me that One

Eye can only focus on one thing at a time. Any distraction like a mouthful of seeds in his eye or a mirror reflecting his own eye back at him will break whatever hold he has on his target, which, if they're quick enough, will give them time to escape. By the way, Budgie, that mirror trick was brilliant.'

I looked at Mouse but he said nothing.

'Maybe we should all carry a piece of mirror in case he targets us,' I suggested.

'I don't think he'll fall for that a second time,' Dog said. 'But you never know. Worth a try, I suppose. Anyway, about Pup, we should be prepared to give him a second chance. I've been talking to him, and he seems to be calming down a little. I think One Eye's encounter with you guys has weakened whatever power he has over Pup.'

Dog paused and rubbed his eyes.

'Pup has started to talk more about his past. Up to now, as you know, he just snarled and abused everyone, especially me. We never knew anything about him or where he came from. Now I know how his mother was killed and why he had to come here. Before she died, the home she had was burnt down. Completely. Everything destroyed. How did it happen? I asked him that, but he didn't know. He was too young to remember, but from the way he spoke, I felt he knew a little bit more about that fire than he was prepared to say.'

'You suspect One Eye burnt his house down, don't you?' I asked.

'Well, it could have been an accident. Accidents happen. The worrying thing is that he told me later that all his brothers and sisters died in the fire. He didn't know them. They had all just been born. Pup was part of a litter. He and his mother were the only ones to survive. She was killed shortly after that and now Pup is here. I don't know why, and I don't know how, but One Eye came with him. Why One Eye has decided to allow Pup to live is a mystery, because surely he could kill Pup in an instant. He must need him for some reason, but I don't know what it could be.'

We all looked at each other. None of us could think of an answer.

'One Eye is the only person Pup has ever really known and we all agree that this rat is particularly evil, so it's important we do our best to show Pup that there are other people, better people, who will care for him. Pup doesn't know anything except hurt and sorrow. We must show him another side. A gentler side.'

I felt a tear form in my eye.

Cat stretched herself in front of her imaginary fire and Mouse crunched a seed.

There was something missing. Something wasn't right.

What had Dog said that didn't make sense? What did he not say?

I didn't have time to think about it, because just then Pup strolled into our group and cheerfully said, 'Hello.'

8

The Plan

P up indeed seemed a different character to the bad-tempered tyke who had attacked me and Mouse. You'd think butter wouldn't melt in his mouth.

He smiled sweetly at both of us and said, 'Ah yes, I remember you. I'm terribly sorry about our misunderstanding. I thought you were common thieves, you see. There are a lot of thieves where I come from.'

'Mouse and Budgie completely understand, don't you, boys?' Dog said.

I left it to Mouse to reply to that, but he didn't. He just spat a seed out which landed very close to Pup. I felt I had to say something.

'I'm afraid, Pup, that we didn't give you a proper welcome to our home. I'm sorry about that. We'd love to see you settled in and learning how the place works. I hear you've had a bad time of it.'

Mouse spat another seed. 'Would you care to explain why you set that friend of yours after us?' he said. 'We were nearly killed.'

'I didn't,' said Pup.

'Then how did he know we giggled that time? And how did he know our names?'

'I don't know. I don't remember.'

Both Cat and I had been dazed when we escaped One Eye, so it was believable that Pup would be confused and genuinely unable to remember what he had told the rat. I didn't really think so, though, and neither did Mouse. 'Harrumph,' was all he could say.

There was an awkward silence.

Dog intervened: 'You haven't met Cat yet, Pup. Let me introduce you to another resident of this house. Pup, meet Cat. Cat, meet Pup.'

The awkward silence went up a notch. I felt sorry for Dog.

Cat glanced disdainfully at Pup and flicked her tail. She could still do that and show her contempt even though her tail had been cut short by the foxes.

'A pleasure, I'm sure,' she said. It was obvious that she wasn't taking any pleasure from the meeting. She clearly thought that if anyone should be pleased, it should be Pup.

Pup picked up on this and turned to Dog. 'You don't tolerate cats in the house, do you?' he asked in an unpleasant snarl. 'That's not right. A cat is the mortal enemy of a dog. Everyone knows that.'

He began barking aggressively at Cat who turned her back on him and began licking her paws and showing her claws, which glistened white and were deadly sharp. I had never seen them before and I was glad they weren't on display for my benefit.

Pup saw them and stopped barking.

'OK, everyone, calm down.' Dog sighed. 'Let's talk about the problem.' Dog shuffled to his feet and looked around at each of us. 'I am the only one here who can deal with One Eye. Cat has failed. I'm sorry, Cat, but it's true. Only for Budgie, who knows what might have happened?'

'I was taken by surprise,' Cat hissed. 'It won't happen again.'

'Nevertheless, you fell under his spell. You can't expect to overcome him if you have to wear a blindfold. No, it has to be me. I'm the only one for this task.'

'I can kill him too,' yelled Pup. 'I'm a dog too.'

Dog laughed kindly. 'Course you can. You're a great dog. You can help by setting up the meeting with One Eye while he thinks you're still his friend. Send him to the corner of the garden where the toolshed is. Tell him that Mouse has set up his new home in the back of the shed and that he hasn't had time to build any complicated passageways. He'll be a sitting duck.'

'What?' Mouse shouted. 'I wouldn't be seen dead in that toolshed. You can forget that plan right away.'

'It's not for real, Mouse,' I said. 'Dog is just setting a trap. You won't have to be there.'

'Oh, I think Mouse will have to be there all right, Budgie,' Dog continued. 'If he isn't, One Eye will smell a rat.'

To my surprise Cat started laughing. I'm amazed that I've never heard her laugh before. It was a nice laugh. It made her less scary.

'He probably smells a rat all day long,' she giggled.

Now we had three gigglers. Mouse started and I couldn't stop myself. It would have been more hilarious if Pup had even smiled. But I noticed that his face remained fixed in a grimace. I still wasn't sure about him.

When we calmed down, Dog went on: 'The plan is that we tell One Eye that Mouse is in the shed and unprotected. Mouse, you might be able to build one of your escape routes, but you'll have to hurry. We don't have much time left. We must set this up for later tonight. When One Eye goes into the shed, Pup will close the door behind him. I'll be in the shed waiting. He won't be able to escape. Cat can join me if she likes. Mouse can look on. You'll be outside, Budgie, safe as houses. We'll get him if everyone does their job.'

'Let's go get him,' shouted Pup.

Mouse looked in my direction, shaking his head.

Then I remembered something that had been nagging me.

'Dog, you mentioned before that you may have met One Eye in the past. Is that true?'

'Yes, I think so, although I can't be sure. One rat is much the same as any other rat to me.'

We waited for him to continue.

'Many moons ago, when I was younger and fitter than I am today, I was used by my masters to hunt out badgers and rats and other vermin like that. My little brother and I enjoyed it. It was great sport to us, but of course, now I realise that it was cruel and wrong. I've killed since but only in self-defence. I don't take any pleasure in killing any living creature, but I'm ashamed to say, in those days I did. I took pride in my work.'

He paused for a moment, then went on: 'One day my brother and I were sent in to clear out a large nest of rats.

They were big rats, larger than normal, with what seemed like a multitude of smaller rats teeming about the place. We concentrated on the bigger fellows and took care of them. There was blood everywhere. It wasn't pretty, but we carried on regardless. We turned our attention to the little ones. They proved to be even more ferocious than their parents and they began hurling themselves like a multitude of crazed mosquitoes at our heads and legs, biting with their little teeth, and when they found a grip, they didn't let go. They drove us mad. We killed them and killed them, but still they kept coming.

'My brother fell. A rat locked himself onto his throat. Before I could get to him, his windpipe had been bitten clean through. He was dead in minutes. I can still see that little rat looking at me. One eye had been torn from its socket and lay like a blue marble in my brother's ear. Still, the little rat dared me to finish him off. I was being attacked by other rats, and by the time I turned around, the little one-eyed devil had gone.

'I think we're dealing with the same rat. I think he's out for revenge. He wants me because I killed his family. And that makes us even. I want him because he killed my brother.'

We were all silent. No one had ever heard Dog speak so many words before.

'If you don't want to help me,' he said, 'I understand. This is a fight between me and him. You don't have to fall in with my plan. Especially you, Pup. You're only here a day, after all.'

'Oh, I'm in, Dog,' Pup assured him. 'What about the others, though?'

Pup had the cheek to look at each of us in turn, daring us to disagree.

I didn't like the way this was going.

I didn't trust Pup.

I didn't trust the plan.

I reckoned One Eye had his own plans and they didn't involve his demise.

And why did Dog think that he wouldn't fall under One Eye's spell?

Second Thoughts

I flew to the toolshed. I had never been there before and I wanted to check it out. After all, this was going to be the battlefield and every good general wants to know the lay of the land, where best to place his troops and what his fallback options are, in case things go wrong.

Before you point out that I was not the general in this battle, or even a foot soldier, I will gladly admit that I had not been enlisted. I was to be a bystander. No role except perhaps to record the events and the outcome.

But I wasn't neutral. If my side lost, then I lost too. My life would be in danger. So involved or not, I had a material interest in the outcome of this fight.

I could see why Dog had chosen the toolshed. It was a simple wooden structure, longer than it was wide, with a sloping roof and just one door in the front. There were no windows. Once you were in, there was no way out except through the door. The lack of windows meant that, without a light turned on, it would be dark. Hopefully that would reduce the power of the rat's eye. If he could be trapped in there, it would be a killing ground.

Then I began to see problems. The set-up was so obviously a trap in the making that I doubted One Eye would fall for it. He wouldn't be so stupid as to walk straight into the darkness of that shed just to find Mouse.

With all due respect to Mouse, I didn't think the prize was worth the risk. One Eye could afford to bide his time for Mouse. If we were to believe Dog, and I did, it was he who One Eye really wanted. Maybe he'd risk it to get at Dog but definitely not for a mere mouse.

I smiled to myself. Cat's observation was more astute than she had thought. One Eye would smell a rat even if Mouse was set up as the bait.

Just then I heard a rustling in the leaves behind the toolshed. Maybe I wasn't the only one checking the battleground. I flew cautiously through the surrounding trees, careful not to be seen. When I got to the rear of the toolshed, I could see some small twigs and bits of earth being shovelled from beneath the wall of the shed. Someone was working feverishly. Could it be One Eye?

Then I heard a familiar voice. 'Bait, I ask you. Unbelievable! I end up as bait. Me! May as well be a worm on a hook. Fish food, rat food. No difference. Well, they've another thing coming. Mouse isn't going to die as bait, I'm telling you.'

I laughed and flew down to join my friend.

'Talking to yourself again, Mouse?' I said. 'You know what that's a sign of.'

He jumped out of the leaves with a screech. 'Yowzah! Budgie, you startled me. Don't do that. I'm a nervous wreck. What are you doing here anyway?'

'Just checking the field of battle,' I said and told him what I thought of the plan.

'Do you really think so?' He sounded relieved. 'I'm not good enough for that one-eyed monster. Yes, I can see your point. Just in case though, I'm making sure that I have a way out. Maybe I'm not the main course, but that doesn't mean I'm not on the menu, does it? You see here, the soil is very loose and there's an old crack in the wood that I've made bigger. I'll be able to get out of the shed quickly enough.'

I should have known; Mouse was always one step ahead. His escape route wasn't perfect though. 'What if he has someone posted outside for just such a plan? You'd walk right into another trap.'

'But he's on his own, isn't he? There are no other rats about.'

'You said yourself, Mouse, where there's one, there's two.'

Just then, we heard some voices coming our way.

'Quick, Mouse,' I said, 'let's hide. You never know. Someone else may be checking out the battleground. Someone from the other side.'

I flew into a nearby bush and Mouse scrambled up behind me. The voices came closer, but we couldn't make out what they were saying. Then we saw them. Pup was leading the way, followed by One Eye. Pup was bringing him to the toolshed. That was part of Dog's plan, I suppose, but I couldn't help feeling uncomfortable about it.

'The shed and mumble, mumble, Mouse,' was all I heard.

'What did he say? Did you hear?' Mouse whispered.

One Eye's head shot up and his ragged ears spun and whirled about.

'Sssh,' I warned.

The rat looked around, cocking his head this way and that. Pup was still speaking.

'Sssh,' One Eye said. 'Mumble, mumble, hear anything?'

Pup fell silent, shaking his head. He hadn't heard anything. Maybe it was my imagination, but I could have sworn he cast a worried glance in our direction.

After a few minutes the rat decided that everything was OK, and he and Pup entered the shed.

'Whew, that was close,' said Mouse. 'Let's get out of here.'

'No, you go. I want to see what they're up to. If they spot me, I can easily get away. You might not be able to get down on the ground quickly enough. Go. I'll see you back at the pond.'

Mouse left. I waited to see what would happen. It was a pity that I couldn't make out everything they were saying.

It wasn't long before they emerged from the shed. One Eye was holding something that looked like a bunch of small sticks. He began going around the shed, stuffing them underneath, into the foundations. Oh no, I thought, if he keeps going all the way round, he's going to find Mouse's escape hole.

But just before he reached Mouse's excavations, Pup barked.

He began to urge One Eye to do something, his paws gesticulating earnestly and pointing towards the house. The rat dropped his sticks and hurried towards the house. As they passed me, I heard them talking.

'Cat's tracks, mumble, mumble,' Pup was saying. This was frustrating. I was only hearing small snatches of their conversations.

Then I heard One Eye saying as clearly as anything, 'When my friends arrive, we'll make our move, Pup. Not until then.'

'But what about Cat's tracks?' Pup insisted.

I was hearing everything as clear as day now.

'Never mind that, look around the shed for tracks, if you like. See what you can find. I don't think these tracks can be important.'

They were up to something and Pup was involved. Whose side was he on? Was he a double agent? Playing both sides, or was he completely under the spell of One Eye? I thought this was the most likely explanation. We didn't know enough yet to make any judgements about Pup.

I had to warn Dog and the others. But first, I wanted to take a look at what they had been doing with those wooden sticks. I was about to fly down to investigate when the branches of the tree next to mine started to shake. Two large, hooded crows were sitting in the tree. A pair of monsters, their dead eyes stared glumly at the roof of the toolshed.

But they hadn't noticed me yet. I edged out of the tree and flew away as quickly as I could.

I never had time to find out what those sticks meant.

I would in the end.

10

The Double-Cross

I made my way back to the pond where I'd told Mouse to wait for me.

He was there, sitting in a pile of leaves, chewing and chomping as if he hadn't a care in the world.

'Where are the others?' I asked.

'Dunno.' Mouse spat out one of his seeds.

'Mouse,' I cried, 'you've been back to the house, haven't you? They're my seeds, aren't they? Have you been into the living room? Is my cage OK?'

'Cage is a bit snarled up, I'm afraid,' said Mouse, in his own relaxed way. 'You might want to consider another one. Seed supplies are running low too.'

Another cage, I thought, would be no use to me. All my papers, carefully hidden in the base of my old cage, would be lost forever. If it couldn't be repaired, I would have to find another hiding place for my memoirs and Mouse would have to look elsewhere for his seeds.

'I've been thinking, Budgie.' Mouse put on his serious face.

I'm always nervous when Mouse is thinking. Usually he'll come up with some crazy scheme involving the supply of cheese or seeds or some other food connected to his ever expanding waistline and which, inevitably, will put my life in mortal danger

'I've been thinking about names and why some of us have them and others don't. I'd really like to have a name, Budgie, but I don't know how I'd find one.'

'But you have a name, Mouse. There, I've said it. You're Mouse.'

'That's not what I mean. Mouse isn't a real name. It's a box. Every mouse in the world is stuffed into that box. We are all the same, so we all get the same name. Look at One Eye. Now there's a name if ever there was one. He's not just a rat the same as all the rest in the rat box. He's One Eye. There's no other rat like him.'

'Well, that's something we should be grateful for. I'm not sure we could deal with two of them. One Eye is evil.'

Mouse sighed and shook his head. 'You don't get it, Budgie. A name of your own is a powerful thing. It tells the world who you are. It doesn't have to be evil. There are good names too.'

'Well, you don't want to lose a leg and be called Pegleg, do you?'

Mouse laughed. 'You're absolutely right, Budgie.' He nodded, as if something had just occurred to him. 'Absolutely right. To find a good name you must earn it. I don't know how yet but I promise you I'll earn a good name. A great name, Budgie, or my name's not Mouse.'

He winked at me and we both laughed heartily. No matter what name he might find on our journey, he would always be Mouse to me.

It was time to get back to reality. Mouse's dreams of a new name would have to wait.

'Where are the others?' I asked. 'I've found out some things they'll want to hear.'

Before Mouse could reply, Dog ambled in, Cat following closely behind.

'What things?' Dog asked.

'I overheard One Eye saying that his friends were coming and that as soon as they did, he would make his move, whatever that means. And they were talking about tracks that Cat was making. I couldn't follow exactly.'

'Friends, eh? I don't think old One Eye has many friends. Probably more rats. You'll have to deal with them, Cat. When the time comes, I fancy I'll have my hands full with One Eye.'

Mouse began fidgeting. 'More rats. I told you so, Budgie,' he moaned. 'I told you, didn't I? Where there's one, there's two. That's what I said, didn't I?'

I was about to mention the sticks when Pup joined us, unannounced.

'Ah, everyone's here now. I want to go over the plan again,' said Dog. 'Now, Pup, you've told the rat that Mouse will be in the shed. Mouse, you better get going and make yourself at home. Wouldn't be sporting if you didn't turn up. Cat and I will be along shortly. Budgie, find somewhere safe up in the

trees. There's nothing you can do. And Pup, head back to
One Eye and tell him that Cat and I have gone to the river so
it will be safe for him to get Mouse in the shed. Tell him that
there's been more trouble with the foxes.' He winked at Cat.
'Don't be leaving any tracks now. OK, everyone spread out.
Best of luck.'

I found a secure spot in a bamboo tree. The branches were
strong enough to hold me, but any larger bird would have
a hard time finding a secure place to perch. I didn't want to
be taken by surprise again by crows. The green leaves and
yellow branches were a perfect camouflage for my colouring.
I was quite pleased with myself. I was learning how to adapt
to life in the open.

I saw Mouse disappear down the side of the shed. I kept a
lookout for Dog and Cat but there was no sign of them. No
sign of One Eye either. I found all the waiting tedious. I hate
to admit that I must have dozed off again.

Then I awoke, quite startled.

One Eye was below me, checking out the toolshed. He
was being careful not to make any noise. I hadn't heard him
but somehow his mere presence must have been enough to
wake me up.

He went carefully up to the door of the shed. This was it,
I thought. He doesn't know it, but he's going to walk straight
into Dog's trap. It's going to work.

He stopped at the door and looked around. He stood up
on his legs, sniffing the air about him. He was huge. He
reached up with his two front claws and slammed the door
shut, pulling down the rusty iron latch that locked it firmly.

He was locking everyone in. I knew it. Pup had betrayed

us. One Eye never had any intentions of going into that shed.

What was he doing now?

He had one of those sticks in his mouth. He was striking it against a rock. A match! That's what those sticks were. How could I have been so stupid? Of course they were matches. What else could they have been?

And now he was setting the shed on fire, going around and lighting every match that he had planted so carefully earlier ... and there was nothing I could do about it.

A deathly scream rang out in the trees behind me. I heard noises and voices coming closer and heading towards me. Bushes and flowers were crashing about as if a small tornado was blowing through them.

Two rats came stumbling into the clearing in front of the shed. They carried more matches on their backs and fell, panting, in front of One Eye who was looking at them in surprise.

Then, charging out of the clearing in a streak of black lightning came Cat.

She wasn't locked in the shed. I jumped up with excitement and nearly fell to the ground. You can hardly blame me.

Where was Dog, though?

11

The Showdown

In front of the startled One Eye, Cat snatched the first rat and threw him against the shed. His matches tumbled from his back, spilling onto one of the already lit matches, and immediately caught fire.

It was then I began to worry about Mouse. I had definitely seen him go into the shed.

One Eye turned his gaze on Cat, who suddenly raised her tail and fell to the ground, covering her eyes.

'That's not going to help you,' One Eye laughed.

Then, from behind Cat, Dog appeared.

He was staring directly into the eye. He seemed not to care.

'Maybe I can help you, Cat,' he said calmly. 'After all, it's me this monster wants, isn't it?'

One Eye smiled. 'So, it is you at last, Dog. I've been looking for you a long time. Today, finally, I'll have my revenge.'

'Or maybe I'll have mine,' growled Dog. 'I remember

you, Rat. You killed my brother. I should have killed you when I had the chance.'

'You're right about that, Dog,' One Eye said.

The rat's eye began to get larger. Again, I could feel its power, even from where I was perched. I watched the action as it played out.

Dog didn't flinch. He stared down One Eye's gaze. The eye got even bigger, so big I thought it might explode. The rat flew into a rage. Dog wouldn't lie down. He wasn't buckling under One Eye's glare.

Cat was now dealing with the last rat. She had him in her mouth, making sure she had her back turned on One Eye and not looking at his glowing eye.

When I thought the eye couldn't get any bigger, Dog sprang forward and sank his jaws deep into One Eye. He tossed the rat towards the toolshed. One Eye bounced off the door and fell to the ground. In that same instant, Cat flung her rat at the door. He hit the ground and rolled towards One Eye. The two lay there, dazed, entangled in each other's claws.

One of the matches, which were still strapped to One Eye's friend, suddenly ignited. Then the other matches on his back exploded in a fiery ball.

One Eye screamed and got to his feet, throwing the other rat against the burning shed. Yellow and orange flames spread along One Eye's flanks.

'The pond,' I heard him splutter. And he ran away.

It was a good idea. Jump in the pond and he'd put the fire out. The trouble was, he ran in the wrong direction. He ran towards the house. I followed him. He obviously didn't know where he was. He ran in circles and by running, he was creating a wind that fanned the flames, which were now threatening to overpower him.

He reached the house and crashed blindly through the patio doors into the sitting room. I flew down to see.

My cage was still lying on the floor. In his confusion, One Eye ran straight into it. The door was swinging back and forth as the big rat thrashed about, trying to put the fire out. I don't think he had even noticed that he was in danger of being trapped in the cage.

It was then that I made the decision which still troubles me to this day.

I flew down to the cage and, trying desperately not to set myself on fire, I shut the door, closing the clasp the way Mouse had taught me.

There would be no escape now for the evil brute.

Was it murder?

I don't know.

I'll let you decide.

I watched as he suffered the very same end that he had cruelly planned for Dog and Cat.

In his last moments, he saw me, his mouth twisted in a terrible snarl. He began shouting at me but the crackle of the flames that were consuming him made it difficult to hear. Something about a curse on all our heads, I think.

I heard his last words clearly: 'Pyjama Boy,' he rasped, 'I'll remember you.'

I cared not at all about One Eye. Of course, I would remember him, but I'm ashamed to say that all I could think about at that time were my papers that were hidden in the

cage, burning away alongside that monster.
I would have to rewrite everything.
That was a curse indeed.
And then I remembered Mouse! What about Mouse?
Had he got out of the burning shed?
I rushed back to my friends.

12

Explanations

I found my friends, licking their wounds, outside the toolshed, which had completely burnt to the ground. They were all there, including Mouse who was complaining loudly as usual.

'Leaving me in the shed, I ask you. Who would believe it? I accepted that I was to be the bait. I've seen enough mousetraps in my time, I can tell you. But really, toasted bait, that's a new one. Hey, Budgie. How would you like bait on toast, eh? I suppose you knew about the plan too. The double-cross.'

'I didn't know anything,' I protested.

'Did you know that Dog here had it all planned out? He knew that Pup would betray him, so he fed him a load of lies about trapping the rat in the shed. All the time, he and Cat were waiting outside. Trouble with foxes indeed.'

'To be fair, Mouse,' I said, 'you or I wouldn't have been

able to fight One Eye. I'm sure Dog did everything for the best.'

'I'm truly sorry, Mouse,' said Dog. 'I couldn't risk One Eye using his power to get the truth from you or Budgie. I told Cat to stay away from us in case she fell under his spell again, but I couldn't tell you fellows to stay away. I never know where you are anyway.'

'What about you, Dog? Were you never afraid of falling under One Eye's spell?' I asked.

Dog looked around sadly. 'No, Budgie. I wasn't. You remember all that talk about Cat's tracks. Well, that was just a red herring. I found out what that vet was really talking about. Cataracts. They're things that affect your eyes. You can go blind. At the moment I'm not able to see much, just shadows. That's why Cat went into the clearing first. She had to signal me with her tail, otherwise I wouldn't have known where One Eye was.

'He never realised that I was almost blind and his eye would have no effect on me. Then, once his eye started getting bigger, I could make him out clearly and I was able to pounce.'

I marvelled at Dog's cunning. He knew what he was doing.

'That's terrible news, Dog. What are you going to do about your eyes?'

'Don't worry, Budgie. I'm due to have an operation. That's what the vet was talking about. I just misunderstood. I'll be fine.'

Mouse wasn't happy. 'And Pup? What about him? He betrayed us,' he said.

'Not entirely his fault. One Eye's power was too great for him. We'll have to take care of him. I'm sure he'll be hurting for a while.'

'What happened to One Eye, Budgie?' Cat wanted to know. 'I hope he's dead.'

I told them how One Eye had died.

Mouse started to laugh.

'What's so funny, Mouse?' Cat asked.

'I always told Budgie that there was only one *i* in birdcage.'

There was a moment's silence and then we all burst out laughing.

'That's terrible, Mouse, one of your worst.'

But we couldn't stop laughing all the same.

Budgie's Notes

Dog had his operation soon afterwards. The cataracts were removed and he's fine now.

Pup remained surly and angry for a while but when we told him that he'd have to act as Dog's eyes while the old fellow was in bandages, he began to come out of his shell. Dog was right. Pup had been completely under the control of One Eye. I think he'll turn out all right, especially with Dog to guide him.

Not only was the toolshed burnt to a crisp but also the living room and parts of the kitchen. I've been hearing rumours that we are to move from the house. Talk is of a farm in some place under a hill. That might be interesting. We'll see.

I've seen my cage. It's in bits. I imagine it will be thrown out.

I don't mind. I couldn't bear to spend a night in there, with the ghost of One Eye haunting it. Not even if Mouse kept me company.

Yes, I hope it's thrown away.

BOOK THREE

The Puzzling Dreams

Contents

1

The White Trucks

Pup was barking.

Nobody took any notice. Pup was always barking about something or other.

Cat was stretched out on top of a radiator in the kitchen, one leg dangling over the side. Out for the count.

Dog was covering his ears with his paws, pretending to be asleep, but I could see his newly repaired eyes darting this way and that, desperately looking for some escape from the relentless racket coming from Pup.

I was looking at Mouse who was voraciously chewing something inedible he'd found on the kitchen floor.

For a moment time stopped. Even if we had wanted to, none of us would have been able to hear Pup's barking. All of us had blocked him out. Each of us were caught up in our own little world.

Suddenly Pup stopped barking and we all heard the silence.

Cat dropped noiselessly from the radiator onto the floor.

Dog looked up.

Mouse stopped chewing.

'You hear that?' asked Pup.

I couldn't hear anything, and to be honest, I didn't really care. All our lives had changed since One Eye had died, and none more than mine.

My cage had been destroyed. It was out of use, still lying on the floor of the living room. I was homeless. I know I may have complained a lot about being a prisoner and everything, but it was still a place I could eat and sleep in, have Mouse over for a chat, do a little writing.

That was another thing. My papers had nearly all gone up in flames. I managed to save some of them and now I'm busy rewriting the rest. I don't know yet where I'm going to hide them when I've finished, but that's the least of my problems.

The burnt-out cage meant another problem. I appear to have been declared lost in the fire so now my steady supply of seeds has dried up. Mouse, you can imagine, is most upset. I look at him scratching about for any scrap of food he can find, and I know we are drifting apart. No more night-long sessions of storytelling and songs, eating seeds until we could eat no longer. I was beginning to realise that we had almost nothing in common apart from those seeds.

I was spending more time outdoors, on the wing. I enjoyed flying with my friends, the sparrows. I had learnt a lot from them, enough to survive in the outside world, at least for the moment. I treasured my newfound freedom and independence, and I knew I owed all of that to Mouse. I didn't like that we weren't as close any more.

Winter would be a new challenge. I could feel it creeping ever closer like a big cold beast, ready to grasp everything in its freezing embrace. The trees had already shed most of their leaves and soon there would be snow on the ground. Finding enough to eat when that happened wouldn't be easy, but the danger was the cold. I couldn't survive in low temperatures. I would be forced to stay in the house.

The thought of living once more in the cage where One Eye had perished filled me with dread. I had visions of his ghost coming back to take his revenge. One Eye was frightening enough in real life, I could only imagine how fearsome he might be as a creature from the spirit world.

It didn't bear thinking about.

I wanted to get as far away as possible from that cage, but I couldn't see how that could be done.

I was thinking about all these things when I heard a rumbling noise.

'Surely you can hear that?' Pup said.

'Thunder, I think,' said Mouse. 'Weather is changing.'

'That's not thunder.' Dog was on his feet, jumping up to look out the window. 'Trucks,' he shouted, 'two of them coming up the drive. That's strange. We never get trucks coming to the house. What do you think we should do?'

Mouse gave his weary sigh.

'Do what you always do. Bark the place down.' He winked at me.

'Time to go, Budgie. I won't be able to bear the racket if these two are going to start. See you at the usual place.'

Without waiting for a reply, he was off. Within seconds he had completely vanished. I wished I could do that. I knew, of course, where he was going. We had long ago agreed the game. The third terracotta pot to the right of the front door.

The one containing a rather robust agapanthus – enough green leaves to conceal us both.

It was a game that both of us liked to play. We liked to throw down a challenge. Who would get there first? Invariably I won. The aerial route was always quicker, but that never deterred Mouse. I didn't think that this was a time for games but at that moment I had no choice. Mouse had gone to ground and would eventually show up at the agapanthus pot.

I cheated, sort of.

When I enter an enclosed space, I always make sure to check out the points of escape. I had noted a new crack above the front door, so I darted straight for it, and in an instant there I was, waiting impatiently beside the agapanthus pot for Mouse, who wasn't there.

I had won again.

I saw the two white trucks pull up outside the house. There was some shouting and laughter, doors banging and a horn tooted. Our two dogs were going mad. They were barking frantically, each outdoing the other. The noise inside the house must have been deafening.

Mouse scrambled into the agapanthus, trying hard not to show any sign of his exertions to try and win the race.

'So you made it then,' he said, as if it was he who had arrived at the winning post first.

I've mentioned before how aggravating Mouse could be. See what I mean.

Before I had time to put him in his place, the cat flap swung open and Cat calmly stepped out.

'Over here, Cat. Over here.' We both called out at the same time.

Cat turned and ambled over to us.

'What's happening, Cat? What are those trucks doing here?'

Cat shrugged. 'Seems like we're moving house. Take a look.'

We looked. Chairs, tables and all sorts of lamps and pictures were being piled up in the yard, waiting to be loaded onto the two trucks.

'Where are we going?' Mouse asked.

Cat looked at me but spoke to Mouse in that high-and-mighty tone she sometimes has. She was in one of her moods. 'Might be a bit of a problem there, Mouse,' she drawled. 'Somehow I don't think you'll be on the invitation list. Hard to believe, I know. Who wouldn't want a cute little fellow like you?'

She flicked her tail and walked away without another word.

Mouse stared after her, speechless.

2

Moving

Poor Mouse. I felt sorry for my friend, but Cat was right, and we both knew it. He wouldn't be included in any move.

The questions occupying my mind, though, were entirely selfish. What would happen to me? Did I want to move?

I was already worried about surviving the winter, but I always thought that as a last resort, if things got bad, I would have the house to fall back on. If it was abandoned, what use would it be to me?

Then there was the dreaded cage. Surely it would finally be thrown away. Moving might be the answer to escape that particular curse. I would never have to see the thing again.

That would be a definite plus.

A move might be just what I needed.

'What's up, Budgie? You have that look in your eyes again. You're up to something, aren't you?' Mouse had perked up.

'Just thinking about this move. It might be the best thing to do,' I replied.

'What? Leave me here, all by myself? You'd never do that to me. Would you?'

I decided to have a little fun with him. 'You heard what Cat said. You're not invited.'

Mouse spat an imaginary seed into the agapanthus. 'Lady Muck. What does she know? She probably thinks she's been invited to a fancy ball.'

'Would you want to move?' I asked.

Mouse mulled that one over. 'I dunno,' he said. 'I like new adventures. On the other hand, a move could be dangerous. All these unknowns that you can't plan for. Still, it won't be the same around here with all you guys gone. I'd be lonely. Yes, I think I would like to move but I'm not invited, am I?'

'Have you ever gatecrashed?' I smiled.

Mouse looked at me, eyes opening widely. 'You know, I don't think I ever have,' he said.

Just then, the dogs stopped barking.

'Something's up,' Mouse said. 'Can you see what's going on?'

I don't like to boast but my eyesight is second to none. I'm not Superman, though. I can't see through walls, and all I could see were the boxes being piled up in the yard.

'Do you think they're OK?' asked Mouse.

'Of course they are. I'll go over and check. Stay here. Won't be long.'

I flew back to the house. The whole place was upside down. All the rooms were being cleared of every bit of furniture. Curtains had been stripped from the windows and packed into boxes. The carpets, were all rolled up and taped, ready to be slotted into the trucks. Among the boxes I spotted the dogs. They had been locked into special travel crates which reminded me of my birdcage. Pup looked comfortable enough, but because Dog was so big, he looked as if he'd been crammed in. He didn't look at all happy.

'Are you all right, Dog?' I asked him.

'No, I am most definitely not all right. This is nothing short of torture. I can't move. First thing I'll do when I get out of here, and get out I will, Budgie ...'

I waited but he didn't finish. 'Well, what will you do, Dog?'

'What will I do? What will I do? I'm going to bite someone. That's what I'll do. I've never bitten anyone before, but this calls for a bite. A big juicy one. One they won't forget.'

I had a lot of sympathy for Dog. I was the expert on cages, after all.

'Ignore him,' said Pup. 'He's upset. He won't bite anyone.'

Pup spoke with a confidence I hadn't heard before. I realised then that we would have to listen to Pup in the future. His opinions would matter.

'What's happening, Pup? Do you know where we're going?'

'I hear we're going to a farm. I haven't heard yet what sort of farm it is. It's somewhere under a hill. I don't know how far away but we're supposed to be there before nightfall.'

'Mouse and I have decided to go with you, if that's OK. I'll have no problem flying into one of the trucks, but I think Mouse may have to hitch a ride in your cage.'

Pup smiled. 'Tell him he's more than welcome. Dog tells me he's a great singer.'

The trucks were finally loaded. The dogs were placed in

The Birdcage Papers

one and Cat in the other. Mouse had crawled into Pup's cage and hid himself in the dog's travelling blanket. Mouse wasn't going to get cold.

I flew into the same truck at the last minute.

The doors closed. The truck's engines roared into life.

We were off.

And then someone outside shouted.

The truck stopped. The doors opened again.

Had they spotted me? Had they seen Mouse? Would they throw us off the truck? Was this goodbye to our friends?

When the doors opened, out of the light at the back of the truck, to my horror, I saw it.

My old, battered birdcage, loaded with the ghost of One Eye and other memories, was being thrown into our truck.

I thought I had escaped the cage but there it was, leaning against the sides of the truck, silently accusing me of murder.

I was beginning to wonder if I would ever escape the guilt that I felt about One Eye and my part in his death.

I hoped the farm would bring new stories and help me to forget.

3

The Farm

We arrived at our destination just before nightfall. I couldn't wait to get out of our truck. The presence of the birdcage was overpowering. I felt One Eye crawling all over me, slithering into my brain, turning it against me and making me want to do stupid things.

I knew that it wasn't real. I'm not crazy.

One Eye was dead.

I wanted to see the farm.

It's probably best that I tell you now about the farm. I'll describe it as I know it now and not the way it seemed to us as we emerged from the darkness of the trucks.

The farm is situated at the top of a narrow valley, which is about a kilometre long. A stretch of water runs the length of the valley, fed by streams and rivulets from the hills that overlook both sides of the water channel. On one side of this gorge the land rises steeply, pine trees clinging to the hillside, crawling their way up to the sheer rocks at the top. On this side, a road winds its way along the water's edge, leading to the farm.

On the other side of the road and the water the land rises gently, allowing for several fields of rough pasture before they too give way to the rising hillside. Sheep graze in these fields. At first, they took no notice of us, but we've got to know them now.

The farmhouse itself is unremarkable – a single-storey building with recently whitewashed walls and a slate roof. Two windows on one side of a red front door and three windows on the other stare down the length of the valley as if warning that this is the end of the road, that you should turn back now.

Despite appearances, the road in fact continues – barely a lane, really – until it emerges on the other side of our little valley.

There's a yard to one side of the house and also a large barn.

When the doors of the truck opened, I said goodbye to the others. The agapanthus pot had been packed away in the back. We agreed to use it as our meeting point no matter where it ended up.

I flew out and upwards, looking for a spot where I could get my bearings. Behind the house, facing the southern sun, a few worn-out apple trees struggled for existence in an old paddock, which contained a few jumping fences for horses. There weren't many other trees about. I suppose there were so many in the hills looking down on us that none were considered necessary down here in the deepest part of the valley.

I flew into the yard and settled on top of the barn. Behind the barn were a few more sheds, mostly in need of repair. Still no sign of life anywhere.

The trucks were being unloaded. Crates and furniture were piled up in the yard. The dogs in their cages were making the usual racket. I think they just barked their heads off because it was expected of them. Then I saw a slight movement below me in the doorway of the barn. The noise had attracted someone's attention.

A cat.

A big, scruffy marmalade cat was taking a keen interest in the proceedings. I reckoned he was a male cat. There were pieces of straw stuck to his coat and one hanging from his mouth which he was chewing with a grim determination. I could see him staring at the dogs, a worried frown on his face.

Then Cat, sitting calmly in her cage, was brought into the yard and Marmalade immediately perked up. Yes, definitely a male. Cat had that effect on them.

He stared at her intently and then looked back at the dogs, confused. I could hear him thinking, What's a cat like that doing with those barbarians?

And then, to add to his confusion, Mouse made his entrance. Emerging from beneath the blanket, he began talking excitedly to Dog, waving his little arms about, trying to explain something.

The chewed-up straw fell from Marmalade's mouth. He gazed at Mouse, his mouth wide open, drooling spittle. Something had changed in his face. He frowned and spat on the ground as if he was trying to get rid of a bad taste. I wasn't surprised, Mouse had that effect on everyone.

Marmalade turned his back on the yard and walked away.

Now that Marmalade had gone, I felt it would be safe to fly into the barn and have a look around. So far I had seen just the sheep in the fields and a scruffy cat. I thought a farm was supposed to have more animals than that. Besides, I needed to find a safe place to see the winter out, and the barn seemed the most likely place.

Inside, the barn was dark and dry and, most importantly, warm. Some light streamed in from a row of small windows in the eaves. I could make out several stalls, one of which was filled with manure, from which a spiral of steam was rising into the air. It smelt a bit. There was a movement in the furthest stall and a grinding noise. I flew closer for a look.

A long brown face with two bulging eyes stared at me in surprise. I had never seen one before, but I knew immediately what it was.

A horse.

A great big, bay horse.

4

Horse

'You're a horse,' I said.

I was a little shocked by the sheer size of the animal. I was perched by the side of his stall and I could see the muscles rippling down his neck as he strained to look at me. He had a narrow white blaze running down the middle of his face. Four matching white markings like half-pulled-up socks wrapped around each of the iron hooves at the base of his massive and long legs.

He looked every inch an athlete.

'Well now, that's very helpful and very considerate of you to point that out, but I'm fairly sure I knew that already.'

His voice was deep and rolled along like a musical instrument. I knew immediately that I was going to like him.

'Who might you be?' he asked politely.

And so we began a long conversation. I told him all about myself, Mouse and the others. He listened patiently to everything I said, chuckling to himself when he heard about Mouse.

'What about you?' I asked. 'How did you wind up on this farm?'

'I was born here. Tenth of May. Not telling you the year. I didn't always live here, though. I was famous once.'

He told me that he used to be a racehorse.

'I used to jump over fences and run for two or three miles. It was a great life, and I was good at it too. Won twenty-seven races. Lost a few, mind, but not so many. That's all over now. Mind you, they still ask me to open new supermarkets and things. I get a day out and everybody claps me on the back. I enjoy that,' he said brightly, but I could see the sad glint in his eye. 'You have your memories to hang on to, of course. Some things you can never forget.'

And then a light seemed to sparkle in his eyes.

'I remember one race very well, the Tingle Creek Chase. Funny name. Two miles over thirteen fences. Exhausting, but I was fit and full of confidence. I had a good jockey on board, looking smart in my black and white colours. He let me do my own thing. Sometimes the jockey thinks it's all about him but it's not. It was about me. I made the important decisions.

'I tucked in behind the leader for nine fences. Most of the horses could run at the same speed. It was all about leaping the fences and no one could do that better than me. Four fences from home there were three of us in it, level pegging. I made my speciality killer jump and landed two lengths ahead of the other two. The stands erupted. The roars and the cheering – you can only imagine! I was tingling all over with excitement. The Tingle Creek Chase is right. All I had to do was jump the last few fences and I had won.'

He sighed. 'What a day,' he said to himself. 'I can still

hear the stampede of hooves and the cry of that jockey in my ear.'

I was swept along by his excitement.

'What happened?' I cried. 'Did you win? Did you fall? What?'

'Course I won,' he said indignantly. 'I was a champion. I won it twice. That was at Sandown. I was so good they have a restaurant named after me in Cheltenham. Mind you, Budgie, I don't suppose you or I will ever get to dine there.'

'Wow, I would have loved to have seen that race,' I said.

'Never mind me, moping about the past.' Then he perked up. 'Things could improve around here, now that you fellows have arrived. Just having that marmalade cat for company is driving me insane. He doesn't want to hear about my races. He's completely obsessed with catching all the mice that live on the farm. We'll just let him get on with it. I'm sure you'll enjoy hearing about all my other races. But you better warn your friend, Mouse, that he's in danger. Marmalade has the mice on this farm under his control. He kills just to show who's boss. He has his informers and knows all the habits of the mice here. He won't like a newcomer disturbing all of that. He'll definitely want to get rid of your friend, Mouse.'

But I was thinking about the other twenty-six races that Horse had won and whether I would survive their telling. Despite being excited by Horse's description of his Tingle Creek race, I suspected that the other races wouldn't differ very much. One race was pretty much like the next, in my opinion. Someone won. Someone lost. I was thinking this, and Horse was mulling something over in his long head when a loud bark broke the silence.

'Budgie, there you are,' said Dog.

Dog and Pup trundled into the barn without a care in the world, looking all around them and sniffing out every smell that wafted through the old building. Mouse was clinging to Pup's collar.

'Nice place,' said Pup. 'This should make a cosy winter shelter for you, Budgie. Bit of a smell in that stall over there, though. I'd avoid that.'

Pup was right. I could see several nooks in the beams of the roof where I could easily build a nest. I had never built a nest before. I hoped it wouldn't be too difficult.

I introduced them to Horse. 'He's a famous racehorse,' I said, but I could see that they were unimpressed.

No one said anything. There was an awkward silence.

I was about to tell them about the Tingle Creek Chase when Horse suddenly reared up onto his hind legs and kicked the wooden slats in front of him. The force of those iron hooves and the noise of splintering wood shook my friends. The dogs wanted to bark but couldn't. They didn't know how to handle such a huge beast as this. Mouse jumped from Pup's back and made sure that he was out of range of the flailing hooves.

Then, almost as quickly, Horse calmed down and sighed deeply. He grunted and pawed the straw in his stall as if he had no interest in it. His thoughts were somewhere else.

We all gazed at this magnificent beast with renewed interest and curiosity. We were afraid to say anything to him.

Eventually he raised his head. 'Sorry about that,' he said. 'Must have drifted off.'

I suppose it was at that moment that Horse became our friend. This huge animal, with all his strength, had a vulnerable side just like the rest of us. We were all equal, no matter what our size.

'Do you always do that?' asked Mouse.

'Do what?'

'Well, I thought I heard you say something. But it wasn't meant for us.'

'Yes, me too,' said Pup. 'Sounded like you were saying, "You too, sis, seen nifty."'

Horse dropped his head and sighed. 'I hate to admit,' he said. 'I've been having these nightmares recently. What just happened there? I don't remember. Did I hurt anybody?'

We all assured him that he did not.

'I keep seeing these numbers. Blue numbers flash across my eyes. Two and then two again and sixteen, mainly. Then occasionally fifty comes up.'

'Two, two, sixteen and fifty. Doesn't make any sense to me,' said Dog in his usual calm voice. 'Does it make any sense to you?'

'No, none,' said Horse. 'I've been thinking about it the last few days and the only thing I can come up with is that they may be fences that I failed to jump. I remember the second fence at Cheltenham and the second at Leopardstown. I was young. My jockey didn't have a clue. I only remember that it hurt when I fell.'

I had never heard of these places, but they seemed to be important to Horse and I couldn't help but notice that the jockey was getting the blame.

'The problem is, though, that I don't remember ever falling at any fence number sixteen, and it's impossible to have a fence number fifty. I've never had to jump as many fences as that in a race.'

'Then they must mean something else,' I said.

'Maybe they don't mean anything at all,' Mouse said.

Horse shook his head. 'Oh, but they do. I'm certain of that.'

5

Settling In

It was a pity that Cat wasn't there to meet Horse. I didn't know it then but she had already met Marmalade. I heard later from her that their first meeting didn't go so well.

She didn't like him at all. He was rough, spoke in a funny accent that she could hardly understand and, worst of all, he drooled incessantly, his long, pink tongue hanging down from his gaping mouth. When he first approached her, he dropped two half-dead mice at her feet. It had been so long since Cat had hunted mice that she was shocked by the sight of the two little things squirming on the ground beneath her. All she could think of was her friend Mouse.

She walked away from them as quickly as she could, but Marmalade kept following her. The two little mice escaped. Marmalade took no notice of them, and Cat was glad. So she talked to him and, to her surprise, she began to like him a little.

After that we noticed that whenever Cat dangled her tail, Marmalade was never too far behind. I will never understand cats.

This, though, was good news for Mouse. With Marmalade being so distracted by Cat, he had a great opportunity to explore the highways and byways of the farmyard in safety. In no time at all, in typical Mouse fashion, he knew everything about the place. He quickly struck up a great friendship with the mice who were scattered about the farm.

During this time, we met at the agapanthus pot regularly, just before the winter snows would eventually confine us to our quarters.

Mouse wanted to confide in me. 'Budgie,' he said, 'I'm worried.'

'About what?' I asked, but my heart wasn't in it.

I'm sorry to say I had my own worries. It probably won't surprise you to learn that after I had chosen a spot in the rafters of the barn to build my nest, and barely before I could finish it, that dreadful burnt-out cage was thrown into one of the empty stalls just below where I was building my first home of my own.

It was permanently in my view. To make things worse, my old chimes had been tossed into the cage, and although they were lying, tangled up on the floor of the cage, they still tinkled a few disjointed notes whenever the wind came whistling under the barn door. I had no choice but to spend the winter here, but I was determined to escape come spring. I had to get away from that cursed cage.

Little did I know that spring would bring with it other more complex problems than a few ghostly chimes.

'Are you listening to me, Budgie?' Mouse asked impatiently.'Have you heard anything at all that I've said?'

Of course I hadn't. I felt myself blushing. At times like

these I'm glad I was such a colourful fellow. Mouse didn't notice my embarrassment.

'I was saying that these farm mice are just simply toys for Marmalade. He's playing with them. They're completely under his power. He decides who lives and who dies. That makes me mad, Budgie. I've got to do something.'

'What can you do?'

'I'm not sure yet. We'll have to organise. The young, strong, fit ones will have to be taught some survival skills. I can do that. You know that I know my way around. Had good teachers myself. We'll have the winter to train. I'm hoping Cat will distract Marmalade enough to give us time to get our act together. You won't believe how simple these mice are. I'm going to change all of that.'

Mouse had a new purpose in life. I was happy for him, but I completely forgot to tell him what Horse had said. 'He'll definitely want to get rid of your friend, Mouse,' Horse had warned about Marmalade.

I shrugged. Horse of the nightmares. What did he know? Mouse could look after himself.

Pup was also finding a new purpose in life. He never spent any time around the farmyard. From almost the first day, he was away, snuffling about every field and hedge in the valley. He took a particular interest in the sheep.

At first, they were afraid of him, but he never came too near. Gradually they feared him less, but they became curious and at the same time suspicious of him. When he'd come nearer, they'd spread out and do everything they could to avoid him. He'd crouch down close to the ground and wait until they relaxed and accepted him. Then he'd bark, and whoosh! They'd scatter in every direction. Pup would stay where he was. The sheep would relax again and return to grazing, one eye always on Pup.

He did this for several days until he was accepted and could walk freely among them.

'They're a bit stupid, Budgie,' he said to me. 'But I like them. They make no demands. They want nothing. All they want to do is eat grass, and yet there are foxes and brutish dogs out there who would chase them and kill them just for sport.'

'And you want to protect them?' I asked.

Pup gave me a bashful look. 'Yes, I do,' he said. 'And very soon, we'll have a new generation coming through. Can you imagine, Budgie? Lambs, hundreds of them. Just think how I could train them. I'll be with them from the day they're born. They'll just accept me, and I'll be able to teach them everything they'll ever need to know.'

'What will they need to know?' I asked.

Pup's eyes dropped to the ground. 'Whatever I tell 'em, Budgie. Whatever I tell 'em.'

It took a while, but Pup was destined to become the best sheepdog ever. His flocks always seemed to know exactly what he meant whenever he barked a certain way. Turn right. Turn left. Straight on. Through the gate. They would fall over themselves to please him.

Dog spent most of his time with Horse. Don't ask me what they talked about. They probably told the same stories over and over again, but they seemed quite content in each other's company as they walked about the paddock and the pastures of the farm.

Horse's nightmares never went away. If anything, they got worse.

All the time, the same numbers kept coming up: two, two, sixteen, fifty.

Mouse began to call him the Mathematician.

Cat thought he wasn't right in the head.

No one knew what the numbers meant.

6

Number 235

When winter came, it came gently, as if it was afraid to interrupt our autumn antics. We didn't know it then, but we would eventually pay a hard price for winter's reticence.

While we waited for the weather to decide how best it would hurl its seasonal blasts of snow and sleet, I was pleasantly surprised by the warmth of the barn.

I was able to survive comfortably on just the scraps of the mountain-high stacks of food that were supplied daily to Horse's trough. There was a price to pay, as you might have expected. I had to listen to his racing tales, and as my luck would have it, he had plenty of them.

I won't bore you with them, except to say that I was right – one race was pretty much the same as all the others. Still, I didn't mind listening to him, with his deep, rumbling voice and his mounting excitement as he recalled some particularly difficult fence which he would eventually cleanly jump without a scratch.

I noticed that he always managed to clear these extra-difficult fences. He never mentioned the encounters with the ones where he fell. I don't think athletes like to dwell on failures.

Mouse came to visit, just like old times.

One night he came quite late and attacked Horse's oats with great enthusiasm. It will not surprise any reader that, true to form, he complained endlessly about the quality of the food on offer.

'Not at all like your old seeds, Budgie,' he said. 'Still, can't have everything, I suppose.'

During these visits he kept me informed about his army of mice and assured me that Marmalade hadn't made any move to eliminate him.

'Don't worry, I've plans in place just in case anything happens. Spring will be on us soon and that's when we'll see where we stand. Talking of standing, I think I'll have a lie down. Is that stall over there free?' he asked.

'Yes, just some old apples in it. Gives the place a lovely smell.'

He sniffed the air.

'Ah, that's wonderful and so warm. Almost makes me feel dizzy.'

I didn't know it then but fruit like apples can break down when they rot and release alcoholic gases which can be dangerous for little fellows like us. Before he even got to the stall where the apples were, Mouse keeled over and slumped to the ground.

'Oh, these apples are wonderful,' he slurred. 'Come down here, Budgie, and smell the fragrance. How delicious.'

Needless to say, I didn't go anywhere near him.

Then he started to sing.

'Come on, Budgie, you must know this song.' He belched loudly.

Horse started nervously in his stall, half asleep.

Then Mouse remembered a favourite limerick:

> There was a young mouse who tried
> A lovely green apple and died.
> The apple fermented
> Inside the lamented
> And made cider inside her inside.

He hiccupped and laughed.

'She was a she mouse,' he explained. 'We'll need more of them in the army.' And immediately he curled up and fell asleep.

I relate this story to you because the whole episode served only to wake up Horse, who snorted and kicked the wooden rails of his stall.

'Two hundred and thirty-five,' he yelled.

'What?' I said.

'Two hundred and thirty-five, Budgie.' Horse kicked his stall in frustration. 'What can it mean? Do you think I'm going mad? All these numbers exploding in my head. I wish it would end.'

And then he noticed Mouse, grappling with the straw in the stall next to him. 'Is that Mouse lying over there, in the apples?'

'Yes, that's him. He was singing, but I'm afraid he's fallen asleep.'

'Oh, I'd like to have heard him sing.'

I assured him that he hadn't missed much and then I had a thought. 'By the way, could 235 have anything to do with the lambs we are expecting soon?' I asked.

Horse frowned. 'Lambs,' he said. 'I never thought of that.' Then he shook his head. 'No, not lambs. We've never had more than a hundred on the farm. Can't be them.'

'Go back to sleep, Horse,' I tried to reassure him. 'We'll find out what it all means in the end.'

If you had asked me then what I thought about the number nightmares, I would have told you that it was just a horse's crazy dream. Maybe something to do with fence numbers, as Horse thought, or maybe they meant nothing at all, just a series of random numbers – two, two, sixteen, fifty and now 235.

'Budgie,' Horse said. 'I can't sleep. I've just realised something. It's the numbers. I can see two and two right now, as clear as day. They're blue against a white background.' He closed his eyes and did his best to concentrate. 'Also,' he said, 'they keep moving about, up and down, jumbling up. What can that mean?'

'Are the other numbers all in blue too?' I asked.

'No, I don't think so. Sixteen has no colour at all, fifty is grey and 235 flashes brown, green and yellow.' Horse shook his big, long head. 'I wish I'd never seen or heard of any of these numbers. They're interfering with my sleep.'

My little nest was located almost directly above Horse's stall. As nests go, I admit it was not the best. I thought that building a nest wouldn't be difficult but once I started, I knew it wouldn't end well. I knew about the materials of nest building – twigs, spit, mud and feathers – but in what order?

Then I realised that my nest would be indoors. With no wind to speak of, I didn't have to spit or make mud. I just laid plenty of discarded feathers in each little crack that I found in the timbers. The result wasn't a palace, but I could live with it.

At night I could feel every sigh and breath that the big racer fligaired in his dreams and I can tell you that, despite what he said, Horse never missed a good night's sleep.

But it did begin to affect me.

Just as I was about to doze off, the numbers would pop into my head and that would be all I could think about. Maybe they could be a sequence of some kind.

Obviously two multiplied by two equals four.

Then four multiplied by four equals sixteen.

But sixteen multiplied by sixteen equals 256.

That didn't work. Our next number was fifty, not 256.

I tried every combination I could think of, but I couldn't find an answer. There was no logic that I could see to the numbers. And now to complicate things further, another number – 235.

I hoped Horse would stop dreaming.

7

Spring Lambs

And so we passed the winter planning, training, scheming, dreaming, waiting for spring to arrive. It came, with new buds arriving on the few trees we had on the farm. Days began to stretch and lush green grass was taking over the fields.

I flew over the farmlands, marvelling at the transformation of the landscape. That's when I first spotted the new lambs, four of them walking awkwardly and bleating noisily.

'They're looking for food,' said Pup when he saw me approaching. 'Their mothers are over there. You can hear them calling. I'll have to show them the way. No time to talk, Budgie.' Then he was off, barking gently at the little lambs and guiding them towards their anxious parents.

Pup had found his vocation in life. Good for him.

As the days went by, more and more lambs arrived. I enjoyed going out to see them. I kept count of how many there were, thinking they might be the key to Horse's numbers.

My instincts proved to be right but not in the way I thought.

When I was out doing my routine checks one day, I noticed from afar that something had changed. All the lambs had been painted on one side.

I went down to have a closer look. There were blue numbers on every lamb. They each carried a unique number on their white flanks.

What had Horse said? Two and two in blue against a white background.

I admit I got excited. Surely this was the answer to our puzzle. I foolishly thought that all I had to do was to find the lambs painted two and two and I would crack it.

I searched out Pup and found him sitting happily among a group of about twenty lambs. I told him what I thought.

'Of course, you're right. Why didn't I think of that? All the lambs have identity marks. Some will be kept on the farm, others will go on to market, poor things.' He whispered, 'Don't want to frighten them, Budgie, but these fellows here have been marked for the market.'

'What about two and two? Where can I find them?'

'They'll be in the field nearest the farm. They won't be going anywhere soon. They're twins, you know. That's why they have the same number.'

I headed back to the farm, amazed at how quickly Pup had learnt everything about the flock of sheep. But when I found the lambs, my heart sank. There they were, two and two, with their numbers clearly marked. They looked exactly like each other. Then again, all lambs looked exactly the same to me. I was so certain that I had found the answer to Horse's numbers but now that I had, I realised that the answer wasn't enough. We still didn't know what the other numbers meant.

They couldn't be other lambs. The numbers had different colours or no colour at all. Until we found out what they meant, we were no nearer to solving the riddle.

I would have to talk to Horse again. Maybe if he knew about the lambs it would jolt something in his subconscious.

I found Horse and Dog strolling through one of the meadows. They were talking beside a wind-battered tree that clung to life near a small hillock strewn with rocks.

'Hi there, Budgie,' Dog called out. 'You're looking all excited. You're looking much greener. The yellow fades when you get agitated. It's probably some sort of camouflage thing. What's the matter?'

That was interesting. I hadn't known that my colours could change. I would have to investigate that, but right now I had no time.

I told them what I had discovered, and Horse stamped the ground in anger. I noticed that his skin colour didn't change. Instead, he broke into a sweat.

'Of course,' he said. 'How stupid am I? I should have known that. It's absolutely clear to me now. Blue numbers on white and all moving about. Obvious, isn't it?'

'But what does it mean, Budgie?' Dog asked. 'Does it mean that Horse's dreams are about these two particular lambs, or does it mean that they just represent all the lambs in general? And does it mean they're in danger? Horse hasn't sensed any danger, have you, Horse?'

Horse was sweating even more. 'I don't know,' he said. 'But why would I kick out like that, in my sleep? That's a defensive reaction. I think it must mean danger. I think it must mean these two lambs are in danger.'

'Well, in that case,' Horse added, 'it'll be soon. Lambs grow so quickly.'

I agreed, but I wanted to find out if any of this had jogged Horse's memory about the next number. 'Do you know now what sixteen means?' I asked.

'I think so, yes, now that you've explained the blue numbers. I told you that at first I thought the numbers meant fences that caused me to fall, didn't I?'

'Yes.'

'Well, I think sixteen is a fence that I've always jumped. That's why I never thought of it. It's a famous fence called the Water Jump. Fence number sixteen in the Grand National at Aintree. It's an easy jump. It comes after the Chair, which isn't easy at all. I remember one time I had a very close shave at the—'

'Horse, not now please. We can talk history later. What is so special about the Water Jump?'

'Ah, let me think. Well, in the race you only have to jump it once. It's a low fence, no height at all, but you must stretch as far as you can because there's water on the other side of it. You have to jump at least thirteen feet, maybe more.'

'And that was no problem for you?'

'No problem at all. The water was only a couple of inches deep, so if you didn't make land on the other side, you just splashed into water, which of course slowed you down and might very well cost you the race, but it wouldn't cause you to fall.'

'So why do you think your dream is about this fence?'

Horse scraped an iron shoe against the old tree. He looked at me and shook his head. 'I have no idea, Budgie. All I know is that for the last two nights I've been dreaming about water. I've been dreaming about drowning in water. Water kept coming into my head, but how could a big lug like me drown in a few inches of water?'

8

The Army

I told Pup to keep an eye on Two and Two. I wasn't convinced that they were essential to our mystery, but I didn't want to take any chances.

It was becoming clear that the numbers didn't make up a puzzle at all. What if Horse's dream were a premonition of something that was going to happen in the future? Some sort of warning expressed in numbers. His dream about drowning was prompted by the number sixteen, a water fence. The lambs also had something to do with it, but what?

The next number was fifty, coloured grey. I decided to have a talk with Mouse. He sometimes had the most illogical ideas that you'd dismiss at your peril. Frequently they turned out to be right and made you look like the stupid one.

I flew to the agapanthus pot and waited. Mouse showed up, as I hoped he would.

'How goes the air force?' he asked cheerfully. Mouse was as happy with life as I've ever seen him.

'Fine, I'm fine, but I need to talk.'

'OK, just give me a moment. I'm waiting for my platoons. The first of them should be arriving here any minute now.'

I didn't know what he was talking about. What was a platoon, anyway?

Just then a little face, full of concern, appeared on the other side of the pot and a tiny voice chirped. 'He's here.'

All of a sudden ten little mice tumbled out from behind the agapanthus, smiling and cheering, clapping each other on the back, high fives all around.

Mouse rose to his full height, arms outstretched, calming them down. 'Well done, Platoon B. You're the first home. Winners to get special provisions tonight.'

There were loud cheers.

'Now, back to barracks and get cleaned up.'

Another big cheer and they were gone.

'What was that all about?' I asked Mouse.

'War games. All my platoons are out today. We're having great fun but it's deadly serious.'

Just then another group of mice appeared. There were no cheers this time when Mouse told them they had come second.

'I've got to be going soon, Budgie. What's the problem?'

I told him about two and two.

He nodded. 'Yes, I can see that.'

We were interrupted by a third platoon which trudged wearily and heavily into the clearing. When they too had been dismissed, I told Mouse about Horse's dream and the water jump numbered sixteen.

Yet another platoon, bedraggled and exhausted, struggled up to him.

'What kept you?' Mouse demanded.

'Nothing, sir. Got lost, sir. Sorry, sir.'

'All right, back to barracks.' He turned to me. 'Budgie, I've really got to go. Looks to me like you're on the right track. You just have to find out what the other numbers mean and then maybe everything will be clearer.'

'But I thought we could discuss it. You're always a great help,' I protested.

'Yes, I know, but I've got other things on my mind right now.' There was a worried look on his face.

'Back to the barracks, is it?' I was disappointed in my old friend and I'm afraid it showed in my voice.

Mouse didn't notice. 'No,' he said. 'I have to go back out there. I've lost a platoon.'

I could have kicked myself. What a horrible budgie I was becoming.

'I'll help you find them – you know, Air Force Rescue.'

'That would be great, Budgie,' he said, smiling now.

He gave me directions and told me to make a sweep of the area near the strangled tree. 'That's where they'll be, I'm sure. That lot are always getting lost.'

And then it struck me.

'Mouse, are there ten soldiers in every platoon?'

Mouse nodded. 'Yes. Why?'

'Well, five platoons make up fifty. Horse's fifty! Don't you see?

'Maybe.' Mouse was thinking hard. 'Maybe you're right, but if you are, then what about me? I'm the general. There are fifty-one in this army.'

The day was turning colder. The clouds overhead were

becoming agitated, their white fluffy edges turning into a dirty brown. The weather was changing.

The atmosphere tightened as if an old iron bucket had been placed upside down over the whole valley, fouling the air with its rusty poison. It was hard to breathe. And then it started to rain.

We soon found Mouse's lost platoon and hurried back to the shelter of the barn. Mouse brought the dripping, miserable little mice in to escape the rain, which had now become heavier.

I counted them in.

'Mouse, there are only nine mice here, not ten.'

'There is a tenth but he's in the sickbay.'

'But that changes everything, don't you see? It means there are only fifty in your army, including you.'

I was certain now that I was right. Horse's fifty meant Mouse's army.

'Well, yes, I suppose so. But we'll be back to full strength again in a few days.'

That could only mean one thing, I thought. Something would happen soon. Before the lambs grew up and before that little mouse soldier got out of the sickbay, wherever the sickbay was.

I was sure of it. But what was going to happen?

And I was still no wiser about that last number, 235.

9

Foul Weather

The rain kept coming all day long and into the night. It was relentless. I was glad of the warmth of the barn and the company of Mouse and his platoon.

Horse and Dog also huddled together for comfort, and we passed the time telling stories about Cat and the foxes and the Shadow. Mouse insisted on recounting the tale of One Eye and his gruesome end, much to the delight of his young platoons.

I couldn't help glancing occasionally at the broken cage in the stall below and I could have sworn that it crackled and sparked every time One Eye's name was mentioned. I wondered where Pup was. He had been the closest to One Eye. I had never asked him how he felt about the cage. It was still raining outside, and night was closing in. Pup shouldn't be outside.

A flash of lightning lit up the barn. Dog started to bark. The doors opened and a swirling cloud of rain tried to reach us with its watery tentacles. Pup appeared in the doorway, breathing heavily, drenched to the bone.

Dog ran to him. 'Pup, are you all right? Come in. Quick, someone close those doors.'

Pup came in and shook himself vigorously, spraying all of us in the process. There was no escaping this rain. It would find its way into our very souls if we let it.

We were drenched but Pup didn't notice. He was the only one who was dry and he was blubbering. 'You were right, Budgie. It's Two and Two. Horse's dream is happening.'

'What do you mean, Pup?'

'I only took my eyes off them for a few seconds, honestly. Next thing I know they'd disappeared. The little scamps. I lost them.'

'We'll send out a search party once this rain stops,' Mouse promised.

Pup shook his head. 'That won't be necessary. I know where they are.'

'Well then, why didn't you bring them with you?'

'That's the problem. I can't.' Pup paused and took a breath. 'I tried, I really did, but the surge of water there is too strong.'

Dog became impatient. 'What in heaven's name are you talking about, Pup?'

'Do you know that knoll in the back pasture, near the strangled tree? That's where they are. They've always wanted to play up there. I saw no harm in it. The hill is safe, and besides, they were building up a lot of strength in their legs, chasing each other up the hill. How was I to know?' Pup pleaded.

Mouse threw up his paws in exasperation. 'It's like trying to get cheese from a mousetrap. What's the problem, Pup? Tell us.'

'That hill is completely surrounded by water. It's an island now and the water keeps rising. Two and Two are on it, trapped.'

There was silence in the barn as we all digested this information.

It was Horse who spoke in the end: 'Well, we can't do anything about it now. It's dark and it's still raining. Let's all get some rest, and we'll see what happens in the morning.'

10

The Island

At first light we were all set to go. I was sent to fetch the cats from the comfort of the farmhouse. They wouldn't be pleased, I thought. Mouse dispatched one of his platoon to get the rest of his army. We were all to assemble at the strangled tree.

The rain had eased during the night and then stopped completely.

I was dismayed when I saw the state of the valley. The road was completely covered by water. The normally placid lake was now churning angrily. The usually barely visible streams that fed the lake from the surrounding heights were sending down torrents of dirty water filled with rocks and debris of all sorts. The rain might have stopped for now but there was still plenty of water in the hills that had nowhere to go except into the lake. The water in the lake would eventually drain away at the bottom of the valley, but in the meantime, it was backing up and levels were rising.

When I got to the strangled tree, the others had all

assembled and a frantic debate was going on. The hillock had indeed been cut off by the rising water. The two lambs had survived the night and were screaming for their mother.

'Why can't Horse just walk across to the island and bring them back?' I asked reasonably.

'It's too deep,' Dog replied. 'The ground between the tree and the hillock has collapsed and been swept away by the water.'

'And I don't rate the tree's chances of surviving much longer either,' added Mouse.

'But that's it,' I cried. 'Don't you see? Horse is meant to jump across! It's number sixteen – the Water Jump.'

Horse looked startled.

'What? The Water Jump was different. It was only a few inches of water. This is deep, Budgie. If I fail, I could drown.'

'But if you succeed, no more dreams,' I said. 'You're a champion. If anyone can do it, you can.'

While Horse pondered this, Pup spoke up: 'But let's say he jumps it, what then? How will he get the lambs back?'

'I know,' said Mouse, quick as a flash. 'He'll bring a rope with him. There's one in the barn. We'll hold one end on this side and when they're tied in we can just pull them across.'

'Good one, Mouse.'

'Not so good, Mouse,' sneered Marmalade. 'Have you looked at Horse's hooves? He wouldn't be able to tie a rope around a frightened lamb. Why can't the big brute swim across anyway?'

'I can't swim,' mumbled Horse.

'What?' asked Marmalade.

'I can't swim, OK?' Horse growled. 'Never could. Never had to.'

Marmalade wasn't giving up. 'Then someone has to go with

you when you make the jump.' He looked at Cat and drew himself up to his full height. 'I'll go,' he said.

'Oh, Marmalade, you're so brave,' Cat whispered. She nuzzled her head into him. 'So brave but so foolish.'

While Marmalade was enjoying his moment as the centre of attention, Pup strode forward.

'No. If anyone has to go, it's me. I'm the only one those lambs will trust.' He looked nervously at the churning water. 'Besides, I can swim just about enough to keep their heads above water.'

I don't know who made the decision, but Pup became our chosen jockey. He jumped onto Horse's back and tried to get comfortable, gripping the horse's mane too tightly, which drew some complaints from the big animal. We wrapped a length of rope around Horse's neck, keeping the other end secured to the old strangled tree. When Horse made the jump, he'd bring the rope with him. We were ready.

I was dispatched to the island to warn the lambs that they had to stand to one side when Horse jumped. We didn't want to rescue a pair of trampled lambs. They understood what I was saying, even though the sight of me appeared to scare them half to death. They stood to one side.

I looked back to the others. Horse was charging towards the island. Pup was clinging to his back, eyes firmly closed. Horse built up a head of speed that would lift him into the air and take him over the water. This would be the water jump of his career. Everyone shouted.

'Come on, Horse!'

'Go, Horse!'

'Jump, jump, jump!'

But I wasn't shouting. I couldn't. The most horrible thought had struck me.

How would Horse get to run like that on the island? There wasn't room. He wouldn't be able to get back.

I finally managed to yell, 'Stop, stop!' But my tiny voice couldn't be heard above the shouting and cheering on the other side.

Horse was flying through the air.

There was no turning back.

11

Rescue

Horse landed perfectly, just like the champion racehorse he used to be. There were great cheers and whooping on the other bank. Horse held his head high and blew a cloud of steam into the air. He looked pleased with himself. Nobody had realised yet that we had a problem. How was I going to break it to Horse?

The lambs cowered behind the rocks. They had never seen anything like this enormous giant of a horse. They now had a new terror to deal with, as if they hadn't been through enough already.

Pup leapt down and pulled the rope from Horse's neck. He quickly calmed the lambs with his gentle voice and explained quietly and clearly what was going to happen. He began tying the rope around the two lambs. 'It'll be alright,' he reassured them. 'I'll be with you all the way over. Just keep calm and keep your mouths closed. You don't want to swallow any of that dirty water.'

While Pup went about his business, I talked to Horse.

'Well done, the racehorse. You were amazing, Horse!'

'Aw, it was nothing really. All in the training. Did you notice the jockey was absolutely useless? No help at all, just like the old days.'

I had to say it. 'How will you get back?'

'I'll just jump back. No problem.'

'But you've no run up. Can you do it from a standing start?'

'What?' He looked around in fear at the shrinking island. He looked at me, his eyes widening in terror.

'That dream. I'm going to drown, aren't I?'

'Not if I can help it, Horse. I have a plan. I'll be back in a jiffy.'

I flew back to the others and told them my news. They were horrified.

'Why didn't you stop it, Budgie?'

'What will happen to Horse?'

'A fine to do, Budgie. Have you told Horse?'

'Yes, and I've told him I have a plan.'

Mouse peered at me. 'I knew it. Budgie always has a plan. Didn't I tell you? What's the plan, Budgie?'

'I don't have one. Not this time. But I know you'll think of something, Mouse.'

'What?'

'It's your destiny, Mouse. Eh, sorry, I mean, General. Horse's dream is coming true. The next bit is up to you and your army, all fifty of you. You'll come up with something. Destiny, Mouse! Destiny!'

I left him scratching his head and flew back to be with Horse.

Pup was barking. 'All set this side. You can pull now,' he called out.

The rope tightened. Pup and the twin lambs plunged into the water. Slowly, they inched their way across the gap that separated us. Dog was pulling for all he was worth. Marmalade and Cat had sunk their teeth into the rope to help support him. The army huffed and puffed but had no real effect on the proceedings. Pup was paddling his legs as fast as he could. The twins tried to copy him.

It seemed to take ages but eventually Pup was scrambling up the other bank and hauling in Two and Two out of the water.

They were safe.

Everyone took a moment to catch their breath and then they all cheered and clapped each other on the back. Another victory.

I could see Mouse glaring at me, shaking his head.

Horse turned to me. 'Well, that was a good job, Budgie. Now what about this plan of yours? It's getting cold again and I can smell more rain in the air.'

I looked across to the other side.

I couldn't see Mouse.

He was gone and there was no sign of his army.

I had to leave Horse on his own.

'Don't worry,' I told him. 'Got to check something on the other side. All part of the plan.'

I hoped with all my being that I was right.

12

The Lasso

When I got to the other side, I discovered why I hadn't been able to see Mouse. He was behind the strangled tree with a large group of his army. They were running up the tree, testing branches, taking measurements and shouting them down to a smaller group who were huddled together, making calculations.

'Ah, there you are,' said Mouse, every bit the general now. 'I have a plan. Told you so, didn't I?'

'Will it work?' I asked, not unreasonably.

'As you say, Budgie, it's all about destiny. If it works, great. If it doesn't' – he shrugged – 'then it's no one's fault. That's how destiny works.'

'What's the plan?'

'Let's consider the problem first.'

I had to stop myself from blurting out, 'Yessir!' Mouse was turning into a real general, full of his own importance.

'We have to get the rope back to the island. Horse must tie himself into it somehow. Then Dog and Pup and everyone here can pull him ashore. Of course it would help if he could swim. That's about it, isn't it?'

'That's about it,' I agreed.

'So, we can't swim across with the rope. Dog is too old. Pup is worn out and the cats wouldn't put their foot in water if you paid them. You were right – that only leaves me and my army. We can swim but we couldn't carry a heavy rope like that, so we'll have to rely on momentum.'

'Look, Mouse, I don't mean to hurry you, but the island is sinking into the lake as we speak. Horse is panicking.'

'OK, OK. I need one of the cats here. Fetch them,' he said to one of his aides. 'I'll show you what I'm thinking once the cats are here.'

Then he was off, scurrying up the tree to see how the rest of his army were getting on. General or not, he was still the infuriating Mouse of old. I could see Horse stamping about on the little island, anxious clouds of sweat rising from his whole body.

At last the cats arrived. 'Can you come up here for a minute, Marmalade?' Mouse called out. 'Unless you're afraid of heights, in which case Horse is doomed.'

The cat flew up the tree like an acrobat, because he could, and because Cat was there, looking on.

Marmalade and Mouse huddled together and began talking intensely, paws thrown in the air, heads shaking, heads nodding, loud shouts of disbelief.

Finally, they came down from the tree and approached me.

'We think it will work, Budgie,' they both said.

'What will work?'

'The plan. You see what we're going to do—' began Mouse.

'Never mind the details!' Marmalade interrupted. 'Just get over to the island and tell Horse to stand as close as he can to the water. Even wading in as far as he can would help. We'll need every yard if the lasso is to work.'

'Lasso, what lasso?'

'You'll see. Hope it works. We haven't had time to practise,' Mouse said grimly. 'Get back to Horse. Tell him the army are coming. About five minutes to showtime.'

I flew back to Horse and told him what I knew. Looking back, I'm glad they hadn't told me the details. Their plan was so crazy that I wouldn't have known how to explain it to him.

I sat behind Horse's ears, and we waited in the water as we had been told to. The water came up to Horse's hocks. We couldn't go out any further.

Then the dogs started barking. They were holding on to one end of the rope which extended up into the tree. I could see Marmalade in the tree, the rope wrapped in the branches above his head, the other end dangling down to the ground. Marmalade began swinging this end of the rope from side to side.

The rope was getting higher with every rotation. Back and forth it swung, faster and faster. Then I saw the army – fifty mice with their tails entwined were clinging to the rope. They were latched to it in a line that extended about ten feet upwards from the end that was swinging back and then coming towards me and Horse.

It got closer and closer, but it wasn't close enough. It was never going to reach us. The plan wasn't working.

Marmalade called out. 'Next swing, Mouse. That's it.'

'You hear that, boys? Next swing. Be ready. You know the signal.'

The rope swung back. The army must have been heartily sick of all this momentum by now, I thought. Then it was coming towards us again. A little before it reached its stalling point Mouse roared the signal: 'GORGONZOLA!'

Suddenly the army of mice dropped into the air. They swung out from the rope in a straight line, extending its length, getting closer to Horse all the time.

A few of the mice had formed themselves into a small hook, a lasso of sorts. The rope, with its mouse hook, flew past Horse's head. Then it reached its stalling point and fell back towards Horse. In an instant the lasso curled itself on one of Horse's ears. The mice were aboard.

Some of the mice hadn't let go of the rope and they stayed connected to the rest of the army by tens of entangled tails, some still swinging in mid-air. The mice on Horse's head were slowly hauling them in, one by one. Marmalade was carefully letting out the rope from his post in the strangled tree. As each mouse untied its tail and dropped onto Horse's head, the rope was getting nearer.

Then the general himself made it.

'Hi there, Horse. Won't be long now. Look, here comes the rope.' He patted Horse's head. 'Careful, everyone. Don't let go of the rope. We're nearly there.'

The army pulled the rope in and wrapped it around Horse's head. Mouse looked at me. 'You realise that this won't be enough,' he whispered to me. 'The dogs won't be able to pull him over on their own. He'll have to help.'

'How?' I asked.

'Horse is an athlete. You saw the way he made that jump. It was magnificent. He'll just have to learn how to swim, and quickly. That shouldn't present any problem to an athlete like him. Teach him, Budgie.'

'That's all very well, Mouse, but I don't know how to swim either. How can I teach him?'

'You know how to fly, don't you?'

'Yes.'

'There you go, then. Who taught you how to fly? Me. And guess what? I don't know how to fly.'

'And where will you be?'

'We'll be on the other side, Budgie. Waiting for you.'

Then he was gone. He scuttled down the rope and began issuing orders to the army. Within minutes, fifty mice were crawling across the rope back to the other side.

They had done their job.

Dog barked, 'Come on, Horse, we have you covered.'

They were all there, holding on to the rope as best they could and waiting for Horse's weight to hit it. Could two dogs, two cats and fifty exhausted mice pull this huge animal through the water?

Mouse was right.

It was impossible.

13

The Strangled Tree

The rope tightened. Horse was tense.

I was clutching one of his ears.

I remembered Mouse pushing me out of the cage all those long days ago. I didn't know the first thing about flying and, you'll recall, I fell more times than was comfortable. Still, I got second chances. Horse would only have one go at this.

I had an idea.

'Horse,' I said calmly into his ear, 'we'll be OK. Just remember your training. Close your eyes and pretend there's a jump ahead. What do you do?'

Amazingly Horse closed his eyes. I knew then I could teach him, but would I be good enough?

'I just push my hind legs, lift my front legs and go. A bit like running upwards.'

'Exactly. That's what I want you to do now, once you're in the water. Just pretend you're jumping over hurdles and keep doing it until we get to the other side.'

'All right, Budgie. I'm ready.'

He was ready. The big, gentle, lovely giant was ready.

But was I?

I could fly away any time I wanted and yet here I was coaching a beautiful, trusting creature how to escape a raging flood. He was depending on me to survive.

'Horse,' I whispered into his ear, 'I'm your jockey. This is your last race. If we don't win, this will be the end for both of us.'

'I hear you, Budgie. I've never had a good jockey yet, but you might be the one. Let's go!'

Horse surged into the waters. The dogs pulled on the rope.

I clung to Horse and shouted my instructions.

'Front legs forward, now back. Back legs forward, now back.'

'I've got it, Budgie,' yelled Horse. 'I've got it.'

We were halfway over when the strangled tree cracked.

I heard the noise as the long-suffering tree surrendered itself to the torrent of water that had invaded its roots. The tree was falling. If it fell into the water, the current would take it towards us.

'Swim, Horse. Not too far to go,' I screamed.

There was a loud snap. The tree broke in two, and the top half fell into the water, leaving behind a stubborn stump. The part in the water turned upside down, righted itself, and then headed directly towards us, its branches looking for trouble.

On the bank in front of us I could see the others, jumping about, yelling, shouting at us, no doubt telling us to get a move on.

The tree was gathering speed. It would be on top of us in moments. Horse hadn't seen it yet. I could feel him fading under me when the first branches hit his side.

He looked around, his eyes wide and startled. I saw the fear rising in them as he realised what was happening. We would be swept down the valley, impaled on the branches of the old tree. I clung on tightly. I wouldn't leave him. I was willing the others on the bank to make one final effort to haul us ashore, but when I looked there was no one there, there was no one pulling on the rope.

Just then the rope around Horse's neck tightened and a huge force pulled us out of the tree's path. In seconds we were scrambling up the bank.

'We did it, Horse. We did it,' I yelled.

But Horse kept stumbling on. The rope had tightened and was still pulling him forward.

'Stop pulling, stop pulling,' I shouted but no one was listening.

There was no one there.

Horse couldn't get a grip. He kept sliding along the wet ground.

We were being pulled slowly but surely towards the broken tree.

I saw the two dogs frantically chewing something in the exposed roots. What were they doing?

Then I saw what was happening.

The rope had lodged itself in a split in the stump of what was left of the tree. It was being pulled through the split and heading out into the water. The other end of the rope was caught in the upper part of the tree which was now being pulled by the force of the water towards the bottom of the valley. We had been saved by the tree but now the very same tree was going to pull us into the water.

Mouse waved at me. 'Stop Horse! Get him to hold back. Sorry, Budgie. We tied the rope around the tree as a precaution but as you can see …'

The rope was stuck in the stump, which gave the dogs a chance to chew through it, but then it would slip and move on again, they'd lose their place and have to start over again. It was hopeless.

Mouse was directing operations, trying to get them to chew it in the same place, but he was losing the battle. His platoons stood around, trying their best to encourage the dogs. Mouse looked worried. He called to me again: 'Try getting Horse to pull back. Give the dogs time to chew through this thing.'

But I had a different idea.

Horse was exhausted. He wouldn't be able to hold back the tree from being swept away by the force of the water. But he could still use his mighty weight.

'Horse, wait. Hold back. Run towards the tree and stop when I tell you.'

He didn't question me for an instant.

'You're the jockey! I hope you're better than the others.'

He ran forward and the rope lost its traction and went slack.

'Now, Horse, Stop! Jump on the rope and wait.'

He managed to get all four of his feet planted on the rope, pinning it to the ground.

'What?' cried Mouse.

'Quick, tell your platoons to get this rope off Horse while it's slack. They were the ones who put it on. Quickly.'

The mice swarmed all over Horse, glad of something to do. They were able to disentangle the loosened rope. It fell to the ground and Horse freed himself. It darted away like a living thing, a snake slithering towards the stump. In a flash it passed through the stump and disappeared into the water. The broken tree was whisked away by the floodwaters.

We had been saved just in time.

'I have to say, Budgie,' Horse said. 'You're the best jockey I've ever had. No doubt about it.'

The army of mice cheered and clapped.

They grabbed Mouse and threw him into the air, shouting, 'General, General, three cheers for our great General Gorgonzola! Hip, hip, hooray!' I could see that Mouse was enjoying every second. 'Three cheers for General Gorgonzola. Hip, hip, hooray.' Mouse flew into the air again.

So, Mouse had found a name for himself at last and it was a good one. General Gorgonzola.

The two cats purred loudly and rubbed against each other as cats do. Pup ran around with Two and Two, barking happily, and Dog sat beside Horse in silent contentment.

I was glad it was all over and I cheered with the rest of them.

But it wasn't over yet.

Budgie's Notes

These notes won't take long. I'm writing them in a hurry.

After the day of the big rescue things settled back to normal. The rain stopped and the water receded. In a few days the road became visible again and the sheep were able to return to the lower fields.

Then just ten minutes ago my life changed.

I was sitting on the roof of the barn when I saw a small dark cloud at the bottom of the valley heading towards us. I knew immediately what it was. A flock of sparrows. They flew down the valley in their lovely formations and settled all around me on the roof, chattering incessantly.

As I am writing this, I can still hear them above me, laughing and calling out to each other. Some of them recognised me from our previous encounters and came over to talk.

After some introductions, I asked them the question that was burning on my mind: 'How many of you are there?'

They had to consult with an older bird. 'According to Number One, we are a total of 234 as of today,' they said.

'Exactly?' I asked.

'Yes, exactly.'

That couldn't be right. If Horse's dream meant anything, there would have to be 235 birds in the flock.

Then, suddenly a light exploded in my head. Bang! The dream number was about me! Brown, green and yellow! The colours in Horse's dream! I was meant to be number 235. It was my destiny. I would become a truly wild bird just like my ancestors before me.

So here I am, beside the old cage where this story began, writing my last piece. I've decided to stuff all my papers into the drawer at the bottom of the cage. I can't think where else I can put them. Besides, the ghost of One Eye, if he's any good at all, might be enough to scare off the over-inquisitive.

I must go now and say my goodbyes to all my old friends. I'll never forget them.

I don't know when I'll be back.

Budgie.

Acknowledgements

I owe a great deal of gratitude to family and friends who helped me push Budgie and Mouse over the line.

Especially Caoimhe and Alan. I hope I haven't embarrassed you guys, but sometimes dads do that.

Big thanks to Peter Brennan, always there with wise counsel. Thanks also to Gerard Nolan, illustrator for the birdcage images, especially for his enthusiastic encouragement.

To all at Kazoo Independent Publishing Services, Chenile Keogh for her enduring good humour and Robert Doran for his sympathetic editing and support.